ANTONIO CASSAR

The Walk to the Well Wood

First edition

ISBN (paperback): 978-1-83709-089-1
ISBN (hardcover): 978-1-83709-090-7

Editing by Theresa Hurrell

This book was professionally typeset on Reedsy.
Find out more at reedsy.com

We are all human.
We all call this planet home.
Whatever differences we have, we must come together,
so that our future selves may live in peace..

Author Socials

Connect With Me

Thank you for reading! The journey doesn't have to end with the final page...

Let's Stay Connected

Want more insights, behind-the-scenes content, and early access to my upcoming work? Join our growing community across these platforms:

I share my thoughts, respond to reader questions, and post exclusive content you won't find anywhere else.

Why Follow?

- **Extended Conversations** - Continue discussions about themes and characters from this book
- **Exclusive Content** - Access bonus chapters, character sketches, and development notes
- **Early Announcements** - Be the first to hear about new releases and special offers
- **Direct Access** - Ask me questions and join live Q&A sessions

Your Voice Matters

Your feedback shapes my writing. By connecting online, you become part of the creative process for future works. Your comments, messages, and shares help this story reach new readers who might find value in these pages.

Find Me At:

Use hashtag #**TheWalktotheWellWood** to join the conversation!

Caldaria

The Free lands of Kings and Queens
The Kingdom of Gesantia
The Dreaded Waste
The Guildlands
The Kingdom of Inoria
The Granagrounds
The West Watch
The Republic of Xanathose
The Dwarven Lords
The Great Plains of the Zaerazzi

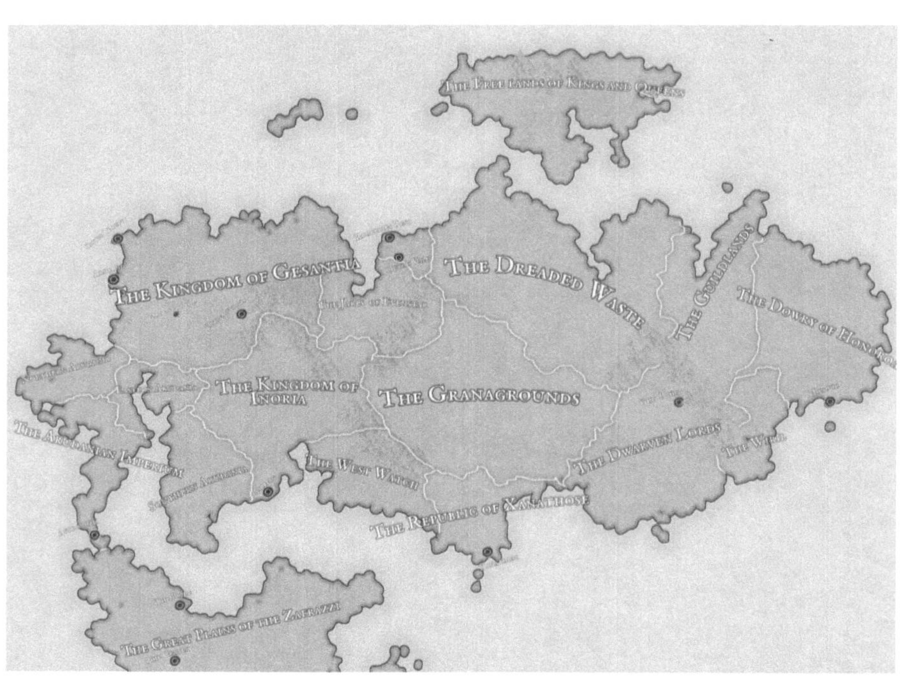

Prologue

Dust billows in his wake as he stumbles through the twisting cave, his torchlight casting frantic shadows on the stone walls. Blood seeps between his fingers where an open wound empties his life force from underneath his steel plate armour. Each labored step sends fresh agony through his side, yet still he turns to look behind, squinting through the haze of earth and the acrid stench of sulphur and iron.

The cold silent darkness behind him gave him hallowed company, but a sight in which he rejoiced, if only there was less of a bitter taste in his mouth. As he ventured further into the depths, now slowing his pace down to avert attention, he noticed the roof of the cave seemed to swallow him as it naturally grew to a hindered height.

The blackness on the wall left a thick stain like a mist enveloping the walls. Any attempt to brighten it from the flickering torchlight ceased. A fools tool, he thought. Maybe it was much more suited to the coward he actually was.

He breathes heavy, catching a few breaths but more importantly his sanity while he retires behind a rock grasping at the cave walls for balance and sits with his knees at eye level. A deep sigh falls over his person, a hollow one at that, one filled with disappointment and failure.

His hand moves from his wound and rests on his legs. They are stained grim, with mixtures of blood, dirt and mucus.

"Fuck...."

He says under his breath while he manoeuvres his head to rest on the rock behind him and lets out tears of pain. Many a time a knight of the order ventures down into the depths of Caldaria in search of artefacts or even more so to the routes of the Well Wood trees. Their roots search the deep depths of the world searching for buried reserves and veins of raw crystallised magic.

This was his mission he told himself. It was until they came across a nest of these… these creatures.

The knight shuddered forward, had he been asleep? After only resting his eyes for what felt like moments. He didn't remember the void of the Dreamlands; everything was so dark down here it was hard to tell. Maybe the pain sent him to sleep. Maybe it was the pain that woke him. The faint glow of the torchlight he had with him is slowly diminishing and in a panicked struggle, he tries to get up. But his legs are numb, numb like the prey in a spiderweb, alive yet laced with venomous sap. His heart pounds against his chest plate but so does the beating of something else. Something grotesque crosses his mind for a moment, but he casts the thought aside while shuddering at what his mind just mustered. He tires no longer, takes a deep breath and takes some parchment and ink quill from his pouch.

'To the finder of my body, I urge you to turn back. I led the knights' order, venturing beyond all waypoints and all known locations, we found that the tunnels fifteen miles from Xanathose stretch beyond any unthinkable distance and deep within these caves lurks the presence of unimaginable creatures. You need to turn back, I am warning you as we had no warning, my unit was surprised and ran, becoming separated. It happened so fast, one group turned back, myself and others turned right from what I recall. Two of my dearest and oldest friends died fending them off. Ripped to pieces while their armour buckled and broke by the sheer strength of those abominations. May they find the crossroads and choose their path wisely and by the gods, if they ever listen again, light the way for them. I only managed to escape by squeezing through a crack in the wall cavity but no one else followed. My only guess is that they died with the others. If you receive this letter, please take it to the High Order at Xanathose and explain to them that we must take measures into sealing the cave entrances otherwise I fear for the world. Men died today fending off a threat we didn't even know existed and if they were to come to the surface who knows what future awaits us. May you find your pathway with vigilance.

Knight-Captain Sir Leywald Huorrace'

His hands grip the letter leaving a smear of blood and dust and mucus upon it and he drops it to the floor. He thinks to himself that he feels a movement. Not within the caves. Not within the dark... No, it cannot be. He cast that thought aside earlier. But now, its happened again. Maybe it's a coincidence. Maybe it's something else...

He unfastens the clasps from his armour rips it from his chest, exhaustion dulling his movements. Carefully, he peels back his blood-stained gambeson and shirt. As the crushed metal is removed, and the fabric brushes against his skin, the wound in his abdomen begins to reopen. Fresh blood welling from the distrubed flesh.

He bleeds ichor now, not blood.

"No... Gods, no... this cannot be happening."

His eyes drop to his stomach. Beneath his skin, something moves. A lump, swimming through his flesh. Small, globular things scurry just under the surface.

He rips the knife from his belt, his breath ragged. His arm follows the shifting lump, muscles coiled to strike.

But another one appears. Then another.

Before he can even think to cut, three more follow.

A bellow of agony and terror rips from his throat as if he weren't alone in the room. By the gods, he wasn't alone in the room.

Then, the burning begins.

Not the warmth of a hearth, but a fire that stings like a thousand wasp stings, like the venom of a scorpion. It burrows deep, embedding itself into him, forging flesh with flesh like molten metal. His blood thickens, clotting like spoiled milk as his body twists in torment, the things inside him thrashing violently.

He screams, his back slamming against the rock behind him, hands clawing at his stomach as if he could tear them out. His arm locks onto a writhing lump— and the knife plunges deep.

The blade rips free. The movement doesn't stop. He missed.

Again, he drives the knife into his gut. Again. And again. A prayer. A plea. A curse.

He screams in defiance, carving into his own flesh, desperate to catch just one

Until...

Until his stomach is nothing but holes.

But there is no pain anymore. Only the sight of ichor spilling onto the stone floor.

That's him. That's his blood. Everything he was, everything he stood for, draining away before his eyes. And he can do nothing to stop it.

His head lulls back against the rock, his gaze drawn to the torchlight, flickering, swaying. Defeat seeps into his hollowed carcass. The real world bends, warping into something distant, something unreal.

His vision falters, dimming with the wavering torchlight.

He lifts the knife, or tries to. The blade trembles in his weakening grip, aimed at his throat. An escape, an end. But his arms fail him. The weight is too much. The knife slips, clattering against the stone.

He couldn't even kill himself.

The torch sputters. The light flickers.

And then, darkness. Only the flesh remains.

1

Sir Osric Erenbell - The Battle

Blood trails stain the snowy blanket on the ground leading to a carcass of a winter bear. Scavengers leave marks and tracks along its fur and the surrounding area. Whatever did kill it?

Maybe wolves, maybe another of its kind overcoming to cannibalism up here this far north, maybe something else. Whatever it is, it marks a meal for any who come across it in this bleak, lifeless season.

Daylight is dying and the cold wind wailed between the trees and then along the not so well-trodden path to be greeted by a sparsely lit torch blinking vigorously in the travellers left hand.

Upon each step, picking it carefully not meaning to step on something under the snow's crust and with each push forward, he brushes away small low hanging branches with his sword, while looking between the small slit in his cloth headwrap, trying to seek out any sign of light elsewhere in this frozen land. The hairs on his arms and legs standing up, frozen, and the weight of the world seems to be crashing against him as the heavy winds push the snow towards the earth. The trees arched and crept with the wind toying with each other as if the fantasy tales of old were true. A flicker of hope licks the air, calling to him like a lost lamb to its mother. There, quietly beckoning to him was the torchlight of a sconce from within a building. Each step tired towards it, now using his sword to help prop him from falling into the snow.

He had made it, with barely a handful of dried fruit and nuts left to his name and even more so a week of not-so-sleepful nights. The sweat on his brow was glacial and his eyelids heavy, nearly ready for sleep and feet battered with sores new and old desperate for rest and attention. Beyond the company of the trees, he steps onto solid ground, reaching the light source he had seen along his weary travels. At the foot of a large wooden hall stands a door about six feet high decorated with owl carvings, runic symbols and a sign saying, "Rookeries Rest". He eagerly presses against the frame with his shoulder almost falling into the well-warmed room. While lowering his head just a fraction under the sturdy wooden beams he stabs his torch into the snow and begins to take his gloves off. Instantly his senses are ignited, baked bread lingers like a lost spirit in the air. His stomach growls eagerly for the taste of the bubbling goulash or stew that fills the air from the fire. Strong, sturdy beams decorate the ceiling as the oak wood creeks as his weighted heavy boots trape across the floor. Chairs hang off the walls, put away for the periods less busy, leaving only a handful tossed about the place. And a few lost souls mind their business sinking their sorrow into whatever lurks inside their tankards "Well, you must be Sir Osric, we have been expecting you. " A young woman with straw-like mousy hair and ragged woollen clothing courtesies and turns to walk towards the bar carrying bowls of unfinished meals and empty tankards. She sets down her burden, hastily wipes her hands on her apron and pours a flagon of ale in a corroded pewter tankard and sets it down onto a well-worn bench. "I hope your trip wasn't too harsh, the roads are non-existent this time of the year." Her eyes flicker for Osric to sit down and drink. "No ale for me. But I thank you for your hospitality. If you wouldn't mind, I'd like some water and a bowl of whatever is cooking." Osric lowers his finger from pointing at the pot, kicks his boots off and brushes himself down, flicking off the thick layer of snow.

"Certainly, my Lord." A wooden bowl is produced as she shuffles towards the pot. Her dress clings to her legs as she walks, scuffing against them as they scrape across the ground. Osric takes a seat, loosening his sword from his belt and placing it onto the table, sighing with satisfaction. He props his leather backpack against the wall and stubbornly slides to the floor before he can unfasten it, so he repositions it and gains entry. He produces a blue crystal no bigger than his hand and puts it on the table. Inquisitively, the barmaid stares at the gem, alarmed and mesmerised as she walks over with his stew. "My Lord, my apologies if I'm out of line but is that an elf tear?" "Yes. That's right." He thumbs over it and thinks about the old days, scratching the blue lapis lazuli like gems rough hew against his fingertips. He levers his cloth wrap from his head revealing a man with a well-worn face. His eyes grey almost pale white like the moons and his hair, long, brown with flecks of split grey's. "Remarkably heavy for what they are really but a lifesaver if you know how to use them." She smiles with amazement in her eyes. He does not smile, only stares. "My Lord, excuse me for asking but what are you doing in these parts anyway? It is a long way from the Orders Keep. I was only told of your arrival by the Baron himself." She snaps out of her hazed look towards the gem, perching her body on the bench opposite. Osric dips his bread in the broth and let's go until little islands of brown stale pieces bob on the goulash. He dusts his hands into his bowl trying to obtain every delicate morsel into it. "Mayor Goodsberry has sent for aid, a monster hunter, he requested. There aren't many of those left in Caldaria anymore as there isn't much left to slay" She looks deep at him. "The monsters are all dead down south but not in these parts my Lord. Head 12 miles to the glaciers and you'll find sea monsters and werebears and all sorts." Osric laughs. "I'll see what I can do, but I doubt it." Arelle doesn't want to speak out of line. Osric obviously refuses to acknowledge what she has seen. "So why you? What's so special about your deeds that makes the order come?" Osric stares. "About 12 years ago I killed the Terror of Ashbern. Mounted its back and plunged my longsword into its head. Shame, they are graceful creatures, but this one was driven mad with grief."

He turns to his stew. "That was many years ago now though. I am merely months from retirement. A nice castle by the east coast to die in." His spoon dips into the stew separating the meat and softened vegetables from the broth.

"What's your name? "He spoons over some of the bubbled bits at the tops and sinks into the sunken meat at the bottom.

"Arelle, my Lord."

His eyes relax and go back towards the gem.

"Arelle. Do you mind if I ponder? It helps me reflect on what is to come and what is to possibly transpire?"

Arelle nods, with which he then removes his hand from the spoon, and very gently runs his thumb over the stone. Like deep arteries of blood pumping around a body, the very magical energies contained within the gem pump in a chaotic fashion. They twirl and twist, separate and combine. Like rivers of sprites dancing to tunes of old. He snatched his hand away from the gem, confused deep with heavy breath and his eyes met hers. Arelle's face drops. She hunches her shoulders and hesitates to talk at first.

"What.... what did you see?"

Osric, stern and back straight, continues to stare at her from eye to eye. Overcome with what feels like the aftermath of a marathon sprint. Images flood into his mind, some of futures to come, some are futures past. But one thing was clear, a baby is a huge part of this vision. One that plagued even Osrics thoughts, a man who has seen so much already.

Osric sighs.

"Death"

2

Lady Alayna Astravix - The Hunted and the Hunter

"Oh, quit your moving! You need to keep still. I cannot fit your dress!"

Alayna's mother, Arrabella, manoeuvres herself around her daughter pondering over her outfit and makeup. Alayna was a young girl with blazing golden hair, wavy strands like the forks of the rivers in Sera. It sat atop her head proud and regal while her beautiful face adorned a button like nose and mesmerising shimmers in her blue eyes. Her slender young body stood sheepishly amongst the small crowd of maids with her mother weaving between them. "No no it just won't do!" Arrabella snaps her fingers. "A pink one!" Some maids scurry off rummaging in a large ivory coloured wardrobe and swiftly bring over a light pink gown with silken embroidery and the finest of embedded gems. Alayna sighs. Arrabella was a lady of beauty, like a vintage wine poured into a chalice of crystal overlooking a vineyard while dining on the finest of cheeses. Exquisite. Her long blonde hair was fixed with silver pins and prongs. She wore a beautiful crimson dress adorned with golden embroidery with a black, intrinsically tooled leather belt holding a sheathed dagger. "Oh, quit your sighing and get on with it, it is your choosing day tomorrow. You're not the only girl in Gesantia that doesn't want to do it!" Arrabella straightens Alayna's hair with a brush, pushing the curled twines of elegant blonde hair up to provide volume.

"But mother, I don't want to have a choosing day. It's not fair. None of it is."

A feeling of disgust boils in the room emanating from Arrabella.

"Well tough. It's your duty to marry off whether you like it or not. Your title, your heritage..."

She rolls her eyes, grabbing what youth she has and regurgitating it out in the form of Ill manners.

"Mother, this is meant to be MY 16th birthday not yours. if I want to wear something other than a dress I can and I will."

Arrabella stares at her daughter as she stops everything she does. She puts her arms onto her hips and her fingers roll against them.

"And what will that be? Peasant gowns? Let me remind you that you do represent me and your father?"

She manoeuvres her head to Alayna so that they face each other, a face of thunder, of murder. "Maybe we can ask one of the maids if they would bring you a set of their clothes? Do you know why I say this, Alayna?"

She walks towards one of the maids, grabbing her by the arm. With force, she is dragged nearly being snapped off her feet. The other maids stand back, gasping but making no noise knowing from experience. Alayna shrugs, her eyes reassessing what she has said and pondering back at her mother and reverting to her sheepish state.

"Do as I say, not as I would have done when I was your age. I was on a path to marry a Prince from the Yester Isles."

Alayna sees in her mother's eyes a dream awakened after being asleep for so, so long. They sparkle and dance and she is reminiscent.

"Instead, my father shipped me off to be with your father here. I could have been a Princess then a Queen but instead I'm a Lord's wife."

She grits her teeth, sliding her tongue along the roof of her mouth and the dream in her eyes dies again, just like it did the first time and many times after that. Her claw-like fingers grip deep into the maid's arm, sinking into the flesh and etching out little trenches.

Drops of blood drip on the hard limestone slabs and join the silence as the deaf can clearly hear the pain from the maid's face. She must not make a sound. She knows this. Everyone does. She sighs and taps her foot, biting down on her anger and channelling it into a more powerful vice.

"I like the pink dress mother."

Arrabella dawn's a smile, removing her clasp embedded into the maid's arm. It bleeds with vigour, but the maid remains still.

"Good, you learn fast, keep it that way otherwise your husband may rid himself of you." Alayna looks at her mother and nods.

"Now, the maids will see to it you are ready sharpish tomorrow, some of the Choosing party have already arrived and I would like to see to it that you arrive on time looking...." She pauses, searching for the word on the tip of her tongue.

"Dazzling. Okay?"

Arrabella looks around the room, looking at everyone closely and then releasing a delayed smile. Alayna toes the floor, barely listening.

"Yes mother"

She lifts her head and just stares at the door and with it her mother leaves in a hurry, strutting towards it with two maids following her with a fan in hand. The door closes.

"She's such a bitch."

Alayna lunges to comfort the maid dripping with blood.

"Are you alright Ezra?"

Ezra wipes the now unblocked tear ducts away smudging fresh blood against her brow. "I'm fine mam" the maid weeps.

"The likes of us know how to keep quiet, else it's worse. She toys with those who snivel mam, it's best to be hush."

She turns to Alayna

"Your ma' isn't the forgivin' type."

One of the older maids, Martha, follows Alayna's path, grabbing some linen and wrapping it around Ezra's arm.

"There there dear, when you get home make sure to mix some potted marigold root with some water, boil then soak."

Martha turns to Alayna.

"We better get ready for tomorrow and tidy all of this up before she gets back, or she might really hurt someone."

Martha was an old woman with stringy hair combed and swirled into a bun. It sat atop her head almost like a hat. Her tired sun kissed dark skin was old and worn like a leather rag. Her back arched as she walked, desperately trying to carry her weight but failing from the toil of so many years. She dragged her tired feet, tending to Ezra's wound. Ezra was a young girl about 14, ginger hair like one of the conquered tribes of Gherreli, a tribe of northmen who owned rookeries rest 10 years ago. She was tall and stunningly beautiful.

"I'm not ready for any of this Martha, I'm not ready to be a wife, a mother or anything. I just want to spend time with my friends and live and sleep in my own home, not to be shipped off to a faraway land where I might not even understand their language. I fear for my life. I fear for your lives. You should all come with me when I go. I would treat you well, pay you well, feed you well. You would never go hungry."

Martha, the old maid, strokes Alayna's back for comfort.

"Oh my sweet dear, you have to think about the positives. You can have anything you want, food, delicacies from anywhere, a protective husband who will do anything for you. And plenty more dresses, even more exquisite than these."

Martha grabs some material from Alayna's' gowns. Delicate stitching conjoins fabrics of two materials together and you can clearly see that an attempt to match the colours has not been successful. Martha Smiles.

"Come dear, let's brush your hair and I'll bring you a cup of wine."

Martha moves towards the makeup table and grabs a fine-toothed comb brush. She pours from a jug into a goblet and hands it to Alayna.

"For the nerves dear."

Alayna pours the cup into her mouth, ignoring the obvious vintage that was contained within and choosing only to embrace its outcome. The satisfying burning sensation comes about her throat, and she shakes her head in realisation. Her head stops as she sits and looks at the old, glazed mirror in front of her. Like dusty sheets of folded grey linen only giving a glimpse at her shadow and figure.

"Martha, Can I ask you a question?"

Alayna stiffens into herself. Almost breaking into an anxious mess. She is met softly, however with Martha's motherly voice.

"Of course, dear. I be only ears for you when you need them, you have always known that" Martha says

"Do you think I would make a good wife?"

Her question reaches out, like a hand in the dark. Trembling with a chill about it, hoping for someone to save her from her mind.

"You don't need to be a good wife, you just need to be a good person."

She pauses, carrying her words.

"And you are already there. If the opportunity arose that you would marry a prince after all this, then you would make an excellent queen for that reason."

It hits Alayna's ears, like a string of soft tunes twisting together in synchronism. But the words don't break through the barriers she has built. Not one single word. She only sees her mother putting chains around her ankles, entangling her in the roots of thought and twine of oppression. She would never be a Queen anyway.

She was nothing.

She will always be nothing.

3

Sir Osric Erenbell - Breaking Bread with a Bastard

Morning shines cheer through the undrawn curtains and the sound of the prized local rooster meets Osric's ears. The light trickles against his face as he opens his tired eyes. He stretches out his back moving himself to the edge of the bed. His eyes glare disdainfully, sheltering them with his hand over his brow as he ponders over his leather sword scabbard which houses his family blade.

With a deliberate sigh, he forces himself up, creaking his legs and yawning deeply as he steps towards his armour and equipment. He stands there for a while, eyeing over his belongings wondering whether all this is worth it and if he should just go home and retire early. He shakes his head, knowing full well it was over three weeks travel to get back home. Even if he wanted to go, it would take him far too long to get back.

Osric shuffles through an empty hall and eyes over towards the table he sat on last night. The table is clear however there is what appears to be some parchment tied up with twine. His hands pat his leather bag as he fumbles through his belongings. Everything seems to be in check. Strange. He unravels the twine, unfolding an invitation from Baron Goodsberry.

'Dearest Sir Osric,

My deepest happiness goes out to the world, and I thank the gods you arrived all in one piece and well. My daughter has explained that you are in fact here answering the call I sent a few weeks ago which is excellent, however I must stress that you are in fact, many days late. I have much to inform you of as there have been reports of further sightings and incidents. The creature has in fact killed a farmer about three days ago. A good man and a faithful subject to Rookeries Rest. I apologise to hasten you but please come to see me as soon as you are ready in the morning. I may have some leads to its lair and some ointments you can apply to your blade to make sure to put it down.

Your Friend,

Baron Goodsberry

Baron of Rookeries Rest and protector of North East Gesantia'

The pot still bubbles the goulash in the centre of the room with the embers of the evening's fire still going strong ushered by the bitter morning breeze which seeps through the slit under the doorway, chilling but not enough to warrant moving away. His heavy boots are still wet from yesterday's travel but warm once his feet are comfortably slotted in, which were tended to with ointment and washed after last night's arrival.

Clasping at the door handle he pulls gently, revealing a harsh and bitter site. Stepping into the landscape and pushing through the knee-high snow he wanders over to the town hall across the street. The town hall itself isn't grand but some of the decorative memorabilia that appear to be recent additions shine out more than the woodwork. Stained glass windows tinted with gold leaf and obsidian, beautifully decorated wood chimes garnish the outer wooden decor of wood frames, and a marble carved owl decorates the porch. He walks forward, moving his hand to wield the brass knocker and with a lift and a good thrust he knocks the door and stands back. A moment passes before numerous heavy creaks come from behind the door and the fumbling of keys can be heard.

Osric is welcomed to a well-lit room as the front door opens and standing there about five foot tall upwards and maybe even outwards is a fat man, shaven and broad. He wears refined clothing with a crisp starched frilly flouncy sleeved shirt, large, jewelled rings on his chubby fingers, a feathered beret hat of the purest of jade silks and patched breeches with long leather boots.

"Good morrow my good Sir, how is your mind and soul?" A fat rolled finger presses against Osric's head and then against his metal chest plate, specifically on the sigil of the bear adorned upon it. Osric looks down at his finger, then back at the man in the doorway. An unimpressed look goes across Osric's face. The man chuckles loudly, in an almost theatrical way.

"My apologies Sir, I should really beg for your forgiveness. My name is Lord Goodsberry. I am the Baron of this delightful town and owner and proprietor of many of the businesses and buildings around here."

Osric reaches into his belongings

"I was sent by the order."

Unscrewing a note from his bag while passing it to the Baron. His fat sausages almost caress the note before taking it off him. Baron Goodsberry gasps.

"My goodness Sir Osric! Please come in! Come in and make yourself at home. I will have the kitchen make you some breakfast and we can chat."

Opening the door providing a more revealing look to the interior hallway, Goodsberry steps to the side, beaconing for Osric to come in. A step forward, from the cold milky feeling on his back to the warmth of the hearth from within the Baron's home. The latch swings shut down upon the clasp as the door closes and the wind chimes sound outside from its movement but gently silence as they stop.

"Follow me my good sir".

Goodsberry runs his fingers across the wall as he walks along creaking wood. He stops just before a doorway arch to a well-lit room as a table and chairs sprawl from within. Goodsberry turns, and with a smile across his face continues to walk forwards

"Osric, how is the south faring? Warmer I imagine?"

They both sit down on thick oak chairs.

"You imagine correctly, but I have not travelled over 300 miles to talk about the weather formations of Caldaria, have I?"

Goodsberry smiles almost excreting a laugh. He clasps at a glass flask of what appears to be whiskey and begins to pour into a glass.

"Partake? I only tend to drink when there's guests"

A raised hand at the bottle and with a shaking head for a gesture, Osric refuses the offer.

"Fine, you have it your way. Business is business."

The Baron caresses the glass, fumbling the liquid within it side to side.

"We have had a monstrous creature come into our village of late. It's mostly taken its share of livestock from the surrounding pastures but recently it's had a larger presence in the town."

Osric nods in acceptance, his hand already making notes on a piece of parchment he had laid out ready.

"Not long ago, it attacked one of our famers in the evening, killing him brutally and rendering his wife a widow."

Osric stops writing.

"Is this man buried somewhere, can I examine the body? Tooth marks or claws may give rise to what type of creature I'm dealing with so I can prepare."

"The body was burned sadly."

He takes a drink from the glass, slurs it around in his mouth and gulps it down his throat.

"However, we think we know where the creature is. A couple of days ago a man named Woodbee, one of our hunters, went a bit further north to see if he could spot some elk. Turns out the elk had already been partly devoured as he found the half-eaten carcass." Osric seems a bit confused.

"He found the carcass out in the open? Seems a bit off for a creature to just leave a half-eaten carcass when it's this far north. They usually eat the whole body, bones, and all. That or drag it into a cave?"

The Baron agrees, slurping another sip. Eyes drifting to the warmth of the hearth. "The carcass was just outside a cave to the north of here. With the recent snow fall though you won't be seeing any blood marks or tracks so it's just you and your nose" Osric finishes his notes.

"I've had fewer hints before and found what I was looking for. It's a start."

He stands, tucking his chair into the table and putting his parchment into his satchel. The Baron stares at him in almost a shocked and horrified way.

"You're not going without breakfast, are you?"

Osric makes his way to the doorway.

"I am. I need to get this done before the creature attacks again." slightly confused and irritated by the Baron's apathy.

Goodsberry lifts his hand up and turns to his glass.

"Have it your way Osric. See you soon and I hope it's with the creature's head. I'll be having words with your authorities if so telling them how much of a respectable job you've done and maybe we can come to an agreement on your forward payment from me personally."

He snaps a grin of teeth.

A kitchen maid walks in with two hot plates of food. Bacon, eggs, sausages, and a tray of freshly baked bread.

"Excuse me my Lord."

Osric stands to the side letting her pass. She places the food on the table, courtesies and stands ready.

"Is there anything else I can get for you, my Lord?"

The Baron stares into his glass, swirling it into his hands and then looks down at his food, then her. He smiles again, showing his perfect teeth after a short pause.

"No no, you're perfectly fine my dear. Osric is on the way to deal with the creature now and won't be joining me for company. But leave me his portion in case I get hungry later on." She smiles, courtesies and walks back to the kitchen. "Fantastic arse on that one, don't you think Osric."

Osric, not pleased by the comment, taps the side of the door frame with his hand twice. "I have to go. I have lots to do."

"Fine. May your sword swing well good sir knight."

With his belongings on his back, his sword to his side and some notes on a location, Osric makes ready for the cold snowy landscape outside. A clasp against the heavy oak door as he swings it towards him and exits into the shivering ice that is the north. The Baron chews on succulent fat from some of the bacon on his plate as he stares at Osric through the window.

He smiles, a grim grotesque smile smacking his tongue against his teeth to mop up any stray pieces of fat and dusts off his oily hands, licking his fingers to consume any moisture from the rashers. He gets up, making his chubby legs almost roll across the floor with small heavy strides and he closes the door into the room he is in, with it firmly shut and lock clasped tight. His eyes glare at the table licking his lips like a starved lion, glaring like a deer upon a disturbed bush and begins to eat both meals like a dog devours a plate of hot potatoes.

4

Saracen Murdock - A Man, A Mage, and A Murdock

A thick stone wall surrounds a nestled keep deep within the Dartons bay. Rebels have overthrown the Lord and left his head on a spike for all to see on the gatehouse. Green and bloating, staring out blankly into the hot sun. It drips bile liquid with disgust. A wretched sight with eyes oozing and maggots which wriggle their way around his nose and mouth.

The banner of the fallen tower flies in the castle, draping from the windows and towers. The symbol of the Gesantian rebellion.

Only five months ago, some of the Lordships increased their taxes to unfathomable amounts, crippling the peasants into paying them triple the usual annual amount in a fortnight. Remarkable, it was near the time of the current Queen Claudia's choosing day after the death of her late husband and many a whisper believes that the tax levy was because of that.

Thousands of villagers stood up to their Lords and now a rolling ball of snow avalanches across the Gesantian countryside and outlying castles leaving its stores ransacked and its people either slain or forced to join. Saracen stands six foot tall with a lock of brown mousy hair. His eyes a deep blue, almost as blue as the sky itself and his face beautiful and handsome with some masculine features to it. A chiselled jawline, muscular upper body, and the sturdy structure of an ox. He puts on his metal helmet and flicks down his visor until he hears a satisfying click. A plume of feathers sticks out from the top showing his rank of Sergeant in the Queen's army. Two magnificent red feathers plucked from a Darton Swift and fashioned into an X-like fashion. His metal armour is grey with tinges of gold, a uniform worn with pride and dignity symbolising a true soldier who has had their wits tested. He sits upon a stallion towering with the other cavalry over the infantrymen. The Vanguard. The soldiers of the Queen. These were his brothers, his countrymen, his people. Like him they shared a common goal. To get home. 10,000 strong and able-bodied men stand with shield and spear to the ready and sword at their sheath. Standard infantry wear bucket helmets with chainmail and the tabard of the Queen's spire worn with commitment, passion and hope to serve their country, their Queen and desire to prove their worth and hope for a better life. Saracens commander strides forward on his horse. Adam Bezran, acting commander of the Queen's army while the main army is off on campaign in the south as rebels have surprised the Gesantians in a pincer movement to aim at the beating heart of the country, the capital, Ardland. Adam and this army are the only thing standing between the rebellion succeeding. As if his forces succeed here then they can go on to relieve the capital. Adams' horse almost struts towards the gate, sharing Adams' sass as the shadow of the gatehouse looks overhead. He speaks in a loud booming voice for all to hear. With dagger point to the full stop. "Good morning Gentlemen. The sun is out and shining down upon our faces. I personally would like to head home and dine on my balcony overlooking my beautiful castle and play with my grand-children." He flicks his reins to his right arm and pulls, looking at the castle walls in all its glory. His horse smacks his teeth against the aggravating snaffles. "But unfortunately, I'm here with all of you. As much as I'd like to play games and enjoy the pleasantries." He pauses for a moment, as the anger boils over the cooking pot. "I must beg you to march your sorry asses down those steps, out of the gates and we won't kill you all for treason. I think that's fair considering what you've done to the Queen and her lands? I may even let you off for killing a dear friend of mine"

Adam gestures at the mounted head on a spike. Pfft, Saracen thought. Like he even spoke to the guy before. The guy was a paederast and deserved it all the same. The only reason he was still alive is because he was a devout sycophant who licks the Queen's spittle. Shame about his wife, she didn't deserve what the rebels did to her. But that's not the game here. No one defies the Queen, and these rebels were about to find that out. Walking up into view on top of the gatehouse, a man with a wine skin in hand wobbles his head left to right, pissed as a fart. He swigs from his drink and points with his other hand at Adam. "Fuck off ya little weasel and all yar litttle friends down there. Ya has gut till tha count of tree untal I come down and kill ya all with me bare hands" He lowers his pointing hand, pulls down his trousers and pisses off the side of the wall, swigging the wine skin from his other hand. His aim points at Adam, but his little pecker doesn't make it that far towards the Commander. Adam turns his head and looks at Saracen directly. He nods, giving him the order and then Saracen turns to the men. "Ladders, move up to advance. Archers knock your arrows." The line repeats this order with light infantry moving up to the ladders placed on the ground in front. Every man breathes a sigh, hoping for a ceasefire and not for a full-scale assault on a fortified castle. Archers draw their arrows from their quivers, tighten their strings and take aim to shoot their bows, giving the infantry some cover fire if requested. Adam moves back with Saracen and the other heavy cavalry, turning his horse to face the castle gates once more. His horse sneezes, as it trumpets a restless groan that it wants to ride. And to ride fast. Its hooves scuff the dirt, and it glares down to the ground. "Shoot the fucker. LOOSE." A thousand arrows are fired at the male on the gatehouse. They fly like a swoop of birds to corn, chirping a sound of whistling wind as their elegance glides through the air. Like pouring pepper onto a steak his body is filled with points as he squirms on the floor smacking against it with the force of a thousand rocks. He groans and moans but laughs between his splutters of blood in his throat. Adam claps his gauntlets together, chuckling as he does. He lifts his hand and unclasps his visor, turning his head towards Saracen. "Well, that was fucking easy." Saracen doesn't share the same pleasantries focussed on the task at hand he stares towards his commander waiting for the order to attack. "Infantry continue to advance, let's get behind those walls and open the gates. I want this to be nice and quick. The rest of those fuckers must be inside the keep". The infantry picks up their ladders and move towards the walls, heavily trudging through the mud as they do. They stop before the old grey stone walls, moss covered and damp from the few nights of rainfall like secreted dew from a maple tree. They raise their ladders to the walls and one by one start the ascent to the battlements. Toying with each other to get up first as they are eager for the hunt to be done quickly so they can get home. The soldiers one by one make their way over the walls and out of sight to join the sound of clashing swords and disgruntled noises echoing the air. Saracen listens and watches diligently, surveying the battlefield and forming an assessment based on many years of experience, he adds to the orders of his commander. "All infantry, form up advance, go give your boys some company. Archers stand too. I want eyes and ears on this battlefield. I have a horrible feeling in my gut." The infantry run at double the pace, with horns sounding and the banners of the Queen flying in the air as they do. As they reach the walls, they begin to climb up one by one. But there, the sun reflects off metal pieces in the distance. From behind the western section of the wall marched a troop of men carrying the banner of the broken tower and as the sun continued to beam down on the field, thousands more men began to flood into view. They waited until the Gesantian forces were divided in two before showing themselves. "Fucking rebels. Gods I didn't want to die today. Not here. I'm not fat or old enough yet."Saracen sees the humour in his comment and just can't help himself. "Sir, I have to object to that statement." All the men laugh, as the cavalry unit musters their humanity once more. Adam punches Saracen in the arm, regretting the impact he makes with steel and nods his head at him in jest. "Well, we may as well braid each other's fucking hair back here." He draws his sword. "For Gesantia! For the Queen!" He swings his stirrups up and slams them into his stallion, bolting it forwards. The other men scream in defiance as the last hope of Gesantia charges into an onslaught heading this way. This should be light work, Saracen thought. These were peasants with little training or real combat experience. They may outnumber us, but we have the advantage, we are the soldiers here. As they hurtle forward, galloping in unison with one another, their Archers turn and begin providing a rain of death. Overhead, whistles fly above them as a parade of arrows fired by the Queen's men fly towards the oncoming enemy forces. They bite at them like cockroaches, and with little to no armour or shields they burst like flesh sacks upon impact. Saracen stares down the wood of his Lance, almost feeling it like it's another limb to his body. The gallop of his horse rides in tune with his heartbeat thumping and thudding against the ground as his horse and him ride in tune with each other like a bond you could not break. They breathed and exhaled in synchronism. The other men follow, in a wedge, with Adam at the point of the arrow. Through the slits in his visor, Saracen sees thousands of people wielding whatever weapons they could muster. Unorganised, unranked but unresponsive to the heavy cavalry charging directly at them. You could feel the adrenaline build from the cavalrymen with some releasing a screamed crescendo, supercharging themselves in readiness for battle. Then the men become quiet and focussed. The hooves smack against the ground creating a rhythm, a Hymn of Death as the charge continues onwards. About now that's all you should hear, thunderous hooves of horses settled into a well-practised drill. But the horses were distracted and couldn't stop making noise. Each one snorted, grunted, smacked their teeth against their reins and wriggled their faces. Something was wrong. Something was off. Amongst the unregimented forces in front of them, a figure steps forward. He grasped hold of a silver blade in his write hand and walked without fear in front of our incoming charge. Adam looks back towards saracen, screaming, screaming an order, but in all the commotion, in all the noise of war, he did not hear nor did he clock on to what we was trying to say. The rebel lifts a lapis blue crystal from within his robes and a shimmer of bright light washes over us. His robes, a crimson red, covering him from head to toe. Like light shining through a stained-glass window. The crystal glow emits brightly into our eyes as the horses kept galloping forwards. It pierced the world around the rebel formation leaving a wave of light that flowed down from above. At that point, the realization dawned upon Saracen that Adam was instructed the charge to halt, or at least move in the other direction. But, it was too late. Saracen is dismounted and sent flying through the air as some form of ethereal force erupts from the very fabric of reality in front of them. He had no idea what was going on by the time he made contact with the ground with his horse following him as it slams down on top of him. He had borne the full weight of his horse, with the velocity and sheer mass he had snapped his ribs and broken his collarbone, shattered his ankle and snapped his fibula. The horses and men pile onto each other, collapsing into heaps and crying for help against their agony. It was a mess, a mound of once mighty men surprised and forced into a stack, a sorry sight with many casualties whining between spluttering blood which fills in their mouths. Saracen went under, his vision halted by the sheer amount of weight that now lay atop of him as more horses and men followed. Struggling for air as the force of all the bodies winds his breath and closes in around him. He scratches out to open areas, trying to feel the air between his fingers and gripping on whatever he could find to drag himself out to safety. He pushes himself through, squeezing out, holding his breath painfully as his chest suffocates under its own weight as he gasps for air like a new born foal does after being welcomed into the world. His eyes flick to the oncoming rebels murdering the stack of men, shoving pitchforks and skinning knives into their chest and faces. He watched as some of the Gesantians survived the charge, defending their comrades to their last breath and watched as swords skewer peasants through their abdomen but only to be dismembered by flanking rebels. Their blood, added to the soaked ground, wetting it like a night of monsoon weather. As the battle began to subside, only the groaning of survivors could be heard and the cackling of men loosening the throats of those grovelling to those that injured them and to those that had killed their comrades. Saracen was lucky, as he dragged his body through the mud until eventually he ended up lying next to a dead horse on the ground. But the pain began to become unbearable, and his eyes rolled to the back of his head as he passed out from the pain, which shattered him and his soul forever.

5

Lady Alayna Astravix - Igniting the Darkness

Alayna didn't sleep much last night, her eyes fixated on her choosing dress hanging up on the wardrobe door, glaring at her and judging. The sun was rising, readying the castle for another day of labour. A labour that will sing its songs in the centuries to come.

A choosing was not a dull affair, not at all. Lords and Ladies from across the land are invited to a Lord's castle, where they are given residence for five days where food, drinks and entertainment are on the house. It was full of debauchery and tournaments where knights would prove their worth and metal. Successful victors gain their renown and are granted one wish from the Lord of the Manor, whether that be gold, titles, land or service. The main event of the choosing is on the fifth day, where the Princess or Prince for example, is displayed in front of the court. There, parties from all over Caldaria will bid their goods, service and treaties to wed one of their own to them. Usually, the one who is offered up for wedlock is given the choice, however the final say will always come back to the Lord or Lady of the Manor. This is where alliances are formed or broken. Where treaties are made or destroyed.

Alayna sits up, grabbing a tear-soaked rag by the side of her bed. Her eyes are bloodshot accompanied by grey bags underneath that hang like bats atop of a cave mouth. A sound of shuffling feet is heard as Martha opens the door looking away from the bed purposefully and drawing the curtains.

"Good morning flower"

She circles back outside into the hall and grasps a tray full of freshly baked pastries and sweets.

"The kitchen knows you well. You sleep okay?"

Martha grabs the bed post and slowly sits down on to the bed giving out a satisfying groan.

"Fine"

Alayna replies. A puzzled look stares softly towards her.

"Oh child, please do talk to me. You know I'm always here for you. You know that right?"

Alayna wipes some fresh tears away from her face, her eyes red and inflamed as she looks at Martha.

"I don't want to do this. This isn't fair. It should be down to me"

Martha gets up, grabbing her lower back and the bedpost as she does and shuffles over to sit next to Alayna. Her arms wrap themselves around her like a cocoon and she kisses her on the forehead.

"Life isn't fair honey. Just look at Mumma Martha. I am 79 and still washing dishes and getting you dressed."

She hugs tightly.

"But let it be known, I will always be there with you. Remember my words, my face and write to me when you can."

Alayna stares gloomy at the wall opposite, eyes now chapped and painful from the tears.

"Come with me Martha. Come with me wherever I go. You wouldn't have to do all of this stuff. You could live out your days and I'd give you everything and anything you would ever want."

It came from the heart, like a young girl would say to her grandmother. It was warm and filled with love. Martha caresses Alayna's face. Her old, wrinkled skin chapped and worn.

"You know your mother wouldn't allow it flower. Be strong. Be courageous. You're not a little girl anymore."

Martha lets go of the hug leaving behind a scared child.

"Come now, before your mother comes and flogs us both "

It was meant to be a form of speech, a play with words. But they both knew about the repercussions. Alayna stands shaky and bruised as her bones feel weak and tired from the lack of sleep. She holds back whatever tears she can, trying to muster up whatever courage her body will allow. Walking tirelessly towards her choosing gown, Alaynas unhooks it and hands it to Martha who has her hand held out welcoming it. She sets it down on the bed and takes off Alayna's bed gown and puts on an underlay, wiping her with essence of lavender and a dab of lemon.

She drapes the gown over her head, securing it with a soft silken ribbon that she ties into a graceful bow. Her outfit is completed with opulent accessories: a silver necklace, featuring a striking sapphire at its core, and pearls that gently rest on her ear lobes, glimmering with every movement. Martha begins to brush Alayna's hair. Bright like a wavey golden river with shining waves of light. Her beautiful locks beginning to be pinned up using silver fashioned brooches. As this unfolds, her gaze remains fixed on the mirror. Her eyes and surrounding sockets like the aftermath of a tempest. They are now stained with a purplish gloom as the redness begins to fade, but Martha begins to rub cucumber under them, soothing her eyes, allowing the redness to go down.

The door knocks, a proud and rushed one that cuts its echo through both Martha and Alayna's silence. Arrabella steps in.

"How stunning you are my sweetheart!"

She rushes over and kisses her on her forehead. Her glare swipes up towards Martha. "Thanks Martha, now would you be a dear and clean up the mess in the courtyard. There has been a little accident, but it shouldn't be too much of an issue to clean up"

Martha nods.

"Yes, my Lady."

With tired legs, she shuffles out of the room, moving each step heavily through her strained hips. Arrabella was already dressed. When she originally requested Alayna's choosing gown for day five, she asked her what she wanted. What jewels, what type of embroidery, what type of precious metal for her necklace. The tailor created a masterpiece. But only now, Alayna realised that her mother requested two of the same dress but with a more lavish and idolised approach to her own.

The embroidery was far more delicate, and the silk spun with gold leaf entwined within.

"Do you like it?"

She twirls, letting down her perfectly fashioned wisps of twirled golden hair.

"Yes mother" a drone, of almost automatic reply, slips from Alayna.

"Well? Come! Your suitors are here! All the kingdoms of the Pathlands have shown up! Even the princes of the Yester Isles!"

She holds out her hand.

"Come!"

Her emerald rings shine in the morning sun, piercing Alayna's tired eyes making the bags under them squirm. She stands up, fluffing her dress and walking with her mother, ignoring the extended hand. Arrabellas face grows angry as her eyes follow her daughter, remembering the small betrayal and storing it away inside her. As they hit the hallway, nerves get the better of her with the thought of suitors and pondering strangers. Alayna grabs her mother's arm and walks with her through the castle hall.

Rugs of crimson colour the floor and shields of a setting sun stain them. The symbol of house Astravix. They walk outside into the courtyard and down a set of steps high above the ground. Many guards patrol the castle wearing tabards bearing the setting sun over their chain mail. Their metal helmets, shield and even the metal tips of the wooden spears they carry are polished and gleaming for this special event. Also, there are other men and women who bear different colours. Some carried swords, other carried axes. All from different lavishes of life. One must assume they are from different countries or places. But the one person Alayna sees is Martha, on her hands and knees cleaning up blood from the limestone slabbing of the yard alone and back twisted.

She was singing a lullaby, sweet tunes that a mother would sing to her baby.

Her eyes with broken dreams that haunt her soul.

"Oh, sweet child, we head to the old world. Back up straight and shoes tied tight. Oh, sweet child we head to the old world. Light your torches and stay out the night."

She catches Alayna's eyes looking at her, quizzing her on what was going on. She shakes her head. Defeated stares flood back to Alayna. She sings again, this time scratching the limestone with anger and pain.

"Oh sweet child, we head to the old world. Light up your torches and stick to the path. Oh sweet child we head to the old world. Run down quickly and get to the light of the hearth."

And there, in the corner was a body. The body of one of Alayna's hand maids. It was Ezra. Moved aside from the courtyard to the dirt and left to die like an infected pig. Filthy and desecrated with her throat still congealing, excess blood around one side of her throat. Her legs appeared shattered, probably broken from a fall from height or possibly worse. Her eyes still hold a little spark of life but there is no turning back now, she was paralyzed and not a single soul came over to help her for fear for their own lives. Alayna did not cry this time, for there were no tears to give. She only stared like a lost ghost in a vast sea of stone.

"Come on my dear, we are going to be late!"

Arrabella ignores her daughter's thoughts, knowing full well of her friendship, even adopting the sisterhood she had with those maids. But she spoke clearly, without a tone of interest and with a keen thought to get this done. Alayna turns her face to look back to her mother, her eyes burning with hatred with flickers of red and purple.

"There's my girl. Come on sweet daughter." Arrabella briskly walks, swinging her full hip towards the large keep. Her shoes clip against the hard stone as her head looks over her shoulder, letting her hair flick against the wind. She smiles with her teeth like little needles in her mouth. The castle was regal, adorning great flags of crimson bearing the mark of a star on the horizon. Alayna struggles forward. Unable to catch a breath. Her gaze goes back to Martha, looking at the old woman cleaning up the blood of one of her sisters as she hums a sweet lullaby. Martha turns, her eyes catch

Alayna. Her hand lifts and presses against her heart.

"Go my child, your destiny is not here."

Her eyes look back at the blood-soaked rag. She hums again, continuing the same song as she scratches the stone floor. Alayna pulls herself up, rubs her tearless face, tired and ruined and follows her mother to the keep. They both stand at the foot of the castle with her mother giving her one final check.

"Back straight sweetheart, you don't want to have crooked babies. Also take that ghastly look of your face it isn't attractive at all. Flaunt your hips and walk in like you own the place."

Arrabella thumbs over Alayna's face, wiping away a stray tear that did manage to breach the duct.

"There there. Now do me and your father proud."

Her smile turns to a smirk as the door opens revealing a room of trumpeters sounding Alayna's arrival. A crimson carpet runs on the floor from the door up to the steps where the Lord, Alayna's father Henry, sits on a wooden seat surrounded by subjects discussing, plotting and drinking fine vintage. Her father stands as he sees the door open, and he smiles a warmth that only a real loving proud father could give to a daughter.

"My dearest Alayna, how beautiful you are. Come and sit up here with me."

His voice sings in the castle feasting area, resonating within the reverberative hall. Alayna sheepishly hides her face as she walks through fields of Lords and Ladies. With each step she made, whispers can be heard with glaring eyes appearing behind the guardsmen who stand along the crimson rug; she could see them through the cranks of their formation.

They were talking about her, looking at her, judging her. The men and women of the court and travellers from far and wide see her in the flesh. The Lord's all step to the side, silent and waiting for Alayna to speak. But yet, she does not. Still, she hides her face from sight, bruised and worn, fighting back tears of frustration and anger, while trying to contain her overwhelming anxiety with all the attention on her. She tires up the few steps that adorn the hall before sitting next to her father and as she turns to sit there is a round of applause.

"Silence!" Henry steals the cheer.

"A small toast to this fine occasion where my beloved daughter will choose her betrothed and a bond will form between our house and theirs! Enjoy your evening everyone, and please do enjoy the cheese, I've heard it's a gift from the Kingdom of Inoria. The main banquet will begin momentarily."

An elegantly dressed woman with cyan coloured clothing courtesies to everyone as she snags a young boy, plump and fat, moaning that the food wasn't ready and for a brief moment the attention was away from Alaynas. Henry raises a glass and takes a sip from his goblet. The room follows and continues with discussions and pleasantries.

"Are you alright?"

His eyes ponder over the many people in the hall as they both sit.

"Yes father."

He taps her knee with his large hand and gives it a little shake.

"I'm proud of you, you know? You can have anyone you want; I'll trust you to make the right decision for the both of us as I feel that all who are here would make fine allies in the coming years..."

She nods, averting her eyes from his as he turns to her.

"Here, take my drink. I'll go and get another one. I love you sweetie; you're going to need something to liven you up. If it's anything like my choosing day, I was in the same seat you were in for 12 hours straight."

Exiting his chair, he smiles at her and limbers towards the crowd and disappears amongst the sea of Lords and Ladies. Alayna stares at her hands, holding in the urge to bite her nails as her anxiety has overthrown her. But she gingerly stops. She moved her hair out of her eyes, her gaze lifting to the crowd as they also meet her sight.

Many are staring her way, many with the finest of clothing and sharpest of tongues like serpents. Judging eyes and whispers of rumours spread around the hall, that's what her mind tells her. But, as if destiny itself blew a gust of wind at that main hall door pushing it open revealing a young man, maybe about 18 with black hair, olive skin and a regal gown. His eyes meet hers, as a sparkling set of brown eyes pierce her very essence. Through the mask of finery and neatly twinned hair that hid her emotional anguish, she felt a surge of something never experienced before in her 16 years of being alive. It was stronger than her darker thoughts, which stood out as unfamiliar and powerful. There was a tingling feeling in her stomach.

6

Sir Osric Erenbell - Good Advice, Bad Decision

One foot in front of the other, that's the focus right now. Each step through the snow on uneven ground beneath its canopy. One wrong step and a twisted ankle could ruin the day. A simple yet terrible injury that would render any warrior useless in a fight.

Osric stopped near a tree, his eyes owl the terrain taking in as much detail as possible. Trees lurk into the air, towering over each other with competitive intent and a rocky crag governs the central part of this forest.

The cave opening in the middle of the forest flickers, interestingly, with a sparse lick of a torchlight that summons Osric's presence to it. From within the cave, light can be seen and with it a trail of black stained blood scraped across the rocky floor. Soaked and stained by the carcass of a once graceful creature.

Osric drew his sword and moved gently towards the cave's jaw, looking at the ground for comfortable footing. His sword, a heavy three-foot-long steel longsword, was forged at the mountain of Ghe' Rahn and sown by fire from the belly of this very world. A masterpiece of a construction, made by some of the finest Smith's in the land. Dwarven craftsmanship mixed with Gnomish keen eyes.

Leather wraps bound the handle made of thick dragonhide, indented with strips of a singular piece of Elven tear fixated upon its hilt, gleaming as it entered from the flash of the nearby torchlight. Piercing the air with each step.

The blade itself looked like silk with etchings of a sonnet embroidered upon the metal. An old poem told way before Osric's parents ever were a thought. Told in a language separate from his own, ancient and forgotten.

'That's where the deer was alright'. Osric thought to himself. The trail of blood weaved its way into the cave and out of sight as its presence was averted due to the glare of torchlight from within the maw.

He looked at the lit torchlight confused. No monster knew how to light a fire.

The caves mouth opened upon Osric's arrival, watching his flank until his eyes adjusted to the light and he could see if anything or anyone lurked there. The cave was filled with delicate roots that arched their way down through the rock and into the floor below stretching and entwining with one another.

Each root twinkled like a night filled with stars from the heavens as blue light rushed through its sap. There must be a Well Wood tree nearby, he thought.

The cave started to decline into the earth and as it did the flicker of another torch beckoned Osric to within. There, surprisingly, was a makeshift wooden piece of bark placed in front of a natural entrance to another part of the cave.

No animal or monster knew how to make fire, let alone make a dwelling. Something wasn't right, this must be the wrong place. He sheathed his sword but held his hand close by to draw in case of any surprises and walked towards the humble dwelling.

"Good morning, is anyone home?" A silent pause apart from the slight sound of rustling from within.

"My name is Sir Osric, I'm with the Order. I'd like to ask some questions". His feet spaced apart and turned sideways, his chin rests on the air chiselled and ready.

From within, Osric's ears picked up the faint echo of a baby's cooing. He looked between the cracks of the bark trying to spot what was within. A footstep is heard from behind him.

Osric draws his sword and turns. He side-steps away from a large stone implement that comes crashing down upon the bark door, shattering it and exploding splitters.

Osric presses forwards and swings his sword to meet the stone implement in the air.

There, wielding a primitive axe was a human-like creature, with a strong brow line, a wide jaw, tusks with hooks and rings attached to it, long braided hair and fury in his eyes. An orc.

"Who sent you?" the orc demanded. The orc pushed his weight upon the axe trying to drive it into Osric's chest.

"Baron Goodsberry, he said there was a monster in these parts killing livestock and stealing food. But I must have the wrong cave." Osric pushed his weight against his sword, balancing the strength of the parry.

"I did take those livestock. And I did take those supplies." The orc explained. "But I have a good reason for doing it all."

Osric looked at the orc with surprise. From within the fury of his eyes Osric sees a scared being. A scared orc doing anything he can.

Osric pushed against the axe, lightly empowering his strength as the elf tear lodged in his hilt glows with inate power, shoving the orc out of the way and to his arse. He then sheaths his sword.

The orc in a mad fury gets up and shouts but notices Osric has disarmed himself. He lowers his axe and dampens his fury.

"You're not here to kill me?" The orc asks as he grinds his teeth while gripping the axe with his well callused hand.

"I'm here to kill a monster. Nothing else. Can we talk instead? I'd like to find out what's going on."

"Out here. Not in there." The orc points towards the enclosed area behind the splintered bark door. He walks towards the rudimentary plank and perches against the cave lining next to it with his back.

Osric nods in response, eyes following the orcs' movement with every action.

"Do your talking then human." He scuffs.

Osric cracks his tired back with a large stretch as he lifts his hands into the air. He then folds his arms and props his left leg against the cave wall.

"What are you doing so far up north?"

The orc shudders at the question. The fury in his eyes wells up like dark clouds turning greyer. His head moves more into his chest sinking like he had been asked a question of woe.

"My wife, Tenya, was captured by some slavers and then sold at auction to the highest bidder. That bidder was the Baron. I was then kicked out of my clan until her return, as Pride governs our lives, human."

Osric lowers his brows slightly. "Slavery is banned in the Pathlands. Are you sure?"

The orc grumbles and chews his tongue as he looks towards the cave entrance.

He spits to the ground.

"I haven't seen her yet. But my sources wouldn't lie to me human. They are people of honour and truth. Not like your Kings and Lords." His eyes look back towards Osric with disgust.

"What's inside the cave?" Osric's eyes peer towards the archway of stone.

The orc pushed his arm across the doorway, forming a barrier. He snorts, chewing at his tongue. A flare of hatred fills his lungs.

"My future and none of your business."

Osric levers his leg off the wall and back to the ground.

"I have seen a baby in a vision. One of your kind."

The orc grunts. "Speak, you leave me on bated breath."

Osric casts his eyes down. "You must leave this place when I find your wife. You are all in grave danger."

The orc looks at him in distrust, stitching together his words in his head. "Idle threats mean nothing to me and my kind. Do you understand?"

"You have my word… I will not harm you. I will get to the bottom of this. And your secret is safe with me." Osric points towards the door.

"Urg-Tor. My name is Urg-Tor, human. I am no monster. Just a worried husband and…" He pauses, swallowing his words.

Osric nods.

"I will find out where your wife is and get you some food. For you and your child."

Urg eyes direct their attention towards Osric.

"Your life for this secret human. Your gods won't be able to save you from me if I get my hands on you."

Osric nods. "Like I said. You have my word."

Osric goes into his bag. He fumbles and grasps hold of a heavy object.

The orc hesitant, as sweat drops from his forehead, he lifts his axe in the air slightly grasping upon the hilt as he fashions himself in front of the door frame.

"Here. Catch."

Osric tosses the orc the elf tear from his bag and walks towards the cave entrance. His head looks over his shoulder.

"Give me until the sun comes up again tomorrow and I'll have answers."

Urg catches the crystal and lifts his head towards Osric walking away from him with his back turned.

"If you prove me right, human. If you betray my slim trust for you and your kind. I will make you suffer."

Osric stops and looks back smiling as he nods in agreement.

Urg sighs with relief, dropping his axe to the ground which was fixated to him for the entire confrontation. He, however couldn't help thinking through.

Maybe this one means well. Maybe this one was different.

He stands and then walk towards the splintered wooden door before turning his head to listen to Osrics footsteps crunchy through the snow.

7

Saracen Murdock - Trophies

Saracen awoke to the sound of a man screaming a battle cry. His footsteps charged through the mud, squelching and squeezing it underneath his feet as he moved closer towards him only to be halted by the sound of a skewering of flesh and then groaning to replace it.

This startled him, shuddering a sense of danger down his spine. He followed the sound with his eyes, not daring to move at this point but he did not see through the blue haze that clouded him. Almost like he had spent far too long staring at the sun as the glare pinned at his eyeballs like needles. It was a strange feeling, unnatural, maybe, an after effect of the magic used to cripple his charge, rather than a battle injury - only time would tell.

His body ached like a tired pregnant mother working the fields all day while he felt his body had sunken into the muddy floor. The damp wet earth enveloped his breastplate, soaking into his clothes and skin underneath. At least, it felt like mud anyway, unless he was sitting in a puddle of someone else's blood, or, even more troubling, his own.

"This one's dead too." A scratchy voice pricks the air from behind him.

"Pile him up wiv the others then. The Lord is going to get first dibs on the loot then we can all have our fair share." They sound like peasants, farmers, cobblers, lumberjacks. People with professions who pay the Lord for safety. Ironic that they would end up killing him instead. These were fucking rebels, Saracen thought.

"Your movin that bloody 'orse though mate, I did my back in on the battle."

A deprecated sigh falls over the other as the rebel manoeuvres his body towards Saracen, bending down and placing his hands on top of Saracen's shoulders. All it would now take is a single movement, and a sharp implement may embed itself into his neck.

"Whore Queen looks after her bloody lakkies. Fine piece of metal this is."

Saracen is fumbled upon, as greedy, grubby hands rub against his armour and clothes, prodding and probing with eager fingers as the stench of the man's breath overwhelmingly overpowers the smell blood. He can feel them groping his skin on show, he lies still holding his breath.

"He's gotta be a leader or cap tin or suffink?"

"Nah, he probably just had sex with the Queen. She offers anyone a bitta steel that ejects inside her filthy snatch."

The other voice speaks up. "How many bastards ya think she's had since being married? Two? Three?"

"Probably more."

A snort as one belches and expels snot from their nose.

"She's too busy with her legs open to even care about her country."

The rebel slaps Saracen's metal chest piece then moves his hand up towards Saracen's face, pinching it in between his fingers admiring his perfections.

Luckily, even through his misfortune, the magic that broke reality stopping the charge earlier had also mildly numbed his senses. Without that, his fate may have taken a different path.

"Come on you fuck face; we got more bodies to drag into piles. We don't want the castle stinking of rot, do we? This one ain't going anywhere, we can come back for him later"

The man unclenches his pinch and stands up.

"Alright, but you're moving the next 'orse you lazy bastard."

The two begin to bicker amongst each other as they filter into the distance, leaving a stream of calm as the sound of war can no longer be heard. Only screaming men. Men calling for aid, for help. Others are calling to be killed. Most men in pain fought for the Queen, struggling to breathe through their injuries.

The sounds, however, were drowned out from the laughter of other men, jesting and toying with the dead, or making more dead from the injured few who struggle alone.

Feeling far more alert now after the crazed adrenaline rush, slowly, Saracen moves his left hand to his eyes. He can see the shadow cast in his vision, but that is all. His vision impaired, but he imagined it would get better.

At this moment he felt peaceful and almost trance-like as if in meditation. It may have been a relief at still being alive, surviving the checking after battle, but it almost felt trance - it was difficult to describe. His mind didn't follow his usual path, planning his next move to survive. He knew what the battlefield would look like around him; he had seen many. He took himself away in his mind reminiscing happy times very vividly, perhaps heightened by the magic.

The battlefield however held horrors. Already, the crows feast upon the dead. Maybe a few hours old. They swoop down in murders attacking each other vying for control over the corpses, starving at the sight of their first meal. They have an elegance about them, even though what they are doing is so grim. But such is life. The dead speak no words. They move no parts. A crow is just trying to live.

Saracen doesn't move and lies with his thoughts. Eyes shut and still.

The piles of dead outweigh the injured. Many of the Queen's men scatter the fields only to be dragged through muddy patches and added to heaps of corpse stacks. Some alive as their intestines leave trails across the battlefield only to be followed by carrion birds and the echoes of screaming.

It jolts Saracen back to reality, ripping him away from his peaceful recollection. His eyes seem to glare slightly, and with a squint, he can make out the blood-stained horses carved up in mounds near him. His eyes look down at his body and a sudden realisation hits him. It wasn't mud that he had been laying in.

Vomit spews into his mouth as he flicks away some loose intestines from his chest plate that bait the nearby crows. Their eyes catch the movement and fly to a nearby pile to feast there in peace.

"Little fucker is still alive." Mud squelches nearby, sounding alarms in

Saracen's ears as a brutish looking glare hovers its way towards him.

"Sweet little boy ain't got a fucking clue."

The glare becomes a figure, standing in front of him with a heavy chest breathing insanity over him. He holds a lumberjack's axe and wears an old, rugged face complete with a brown beard and scarred arm, possibly a deliberate roose to make himself look more menacing. The scar was in the shape of the letter M, burnt using a metallic implement. He bends down over Saracen, eyeing up his armour and weapons. Thumbing over his blood-stained clothes and flicking off the giblets that cover him.

"Too small for me. Might fetch me some coins. Might fetch me some coins indeed."

He stands up straight, arching his back to the side as he flings his axe into his shoulder. He raises his axe into the air eclipsing the shine from the sun and pauses his breath.

"No. Please." Saracens words came out of his mouth. Not even a whisper could best describe it.

A failed attempt at mercy. Fate seems to be working in mysterious ways today. The axe comes down, brutally crashing through the air as it slices down towards Saracen.

He tries to roll out the way, but the weight of his armour and the effort of the liquid earth hold him almost firmly to the ground. His arm raises into the air, hoping for mercy, even though it was too late.

Contact was horrifying. Blood spewed out of him and added to the muddy mix he laid in. It cut into his arm, in the middle of his forearm. He screamed in defiance, breaking his meek silence and adding to the cacophony of sounds on the battlefield.

The brute chuckled to his pain. He puts his foot onto Saracen's chest, prying his axe out of his embedded arm and pushing his body even more firmly into the mud. He then sticks it into the ground, covering the axe in dirt that sticks to its dripping like ooze, staring at Saracen whose sight is still impaired. Grinning.

"It's your lucky day sweet boy. I'm gonna let you live. For now."

Saracen raises his unhurt hand with agonising glare

"Please. Please." He pauses between words, swallowing the moisture from his mouth as he focuses away from the pain. Gritting at his teeth as little echoes of agony spit from his mouth.

"I'll just let nature take you instead. Your arm will go green, and you'll come down with a fever. And if you're lucky you will die before the crows peck out your eyes and tongue while you still cast breath."

He raises his axe into the air again, slamming it down towards him this time severing his arm from his body.

"What's your name, pretty boy? I'd like to write it down in my book."

Saracen screams again in defiance, ignoring the question, to focused on the pain which becomes unbearable making his mind hollow and weak. He sputters out a few words, but only verbal gristle comes out. Again, his eyes weaken as his heart pounds onto his chest plate.

"Fuck the Queen."

The man bends down, unstrapping Saracens belt, unhooking his sword scabbard and smiles. He fumbles around in his belongings and finds some paperwork of rank and order.

"Saracen Murdock."

He laughs. "Your father must be a drunk. What a pathetic attempt to name a son."

The brute spits into Saracen's face, he gets up and he walks away leaving him to add to the battlefield filled with corpses and blood.

8

Lady Alayna Astravix - Adorning the Whispers of Affection

The doors close, clasping shut on the thick iron hinges. Standing amongst a crowd of fashioned soldiers bearing crescent gold helmets and purple capes, is a man, no older than eighteen. He is young of face with tanned olive skin and beautiful black hair that would have sat at shoulder length if it had not been tied at the top.

Alayna's Father grasps hold of her and strokes her hand. He looks at her, quizzingly, but her eyes are not interested. She is fixated, mesmerized upon the people who had just entered the dining hall. Or to be exact, that one person in particular who had caught her attention. He is looking straight at her, sending her stomach in knots and her heart racing.

He crosses the woven silk carpet with such grace he almost glides. Such dignity and charisma, clasping his scabbard, fashioning his cape to the side. The crowds mutter and run rings of words with each other. Echoes of voices bounce off walls and shimmer in ears. The talk of Imperial or empire is heard amongst the hushes.

"His Royal Highness, Prince Joseph Loredan the Third of The Arudanian Imperium." The spokesman rolls up his scroll and bows before the Lord and Prince before retiring.

Joseph stops before the steps to the family seats and looks to Alayna's father. "Lord Henry of Gesantia. I am honored to receive your invitation of hospitality and bring you spices and gold as gifts."

A twisted tongue of sounds. Like salt sea air lavishing against a bay of rocky beaches. It had a twang to it, his words, a far-stretched whistle of ways that almost enticed the strongest of men and women. She could feel her heart beating faster at the sound of his voice, strong, regal, and clearly well educated.

He lowers his back, bowing as two soldiers bring silver bowls and place them by his feet. One contains gold jewelry encrusted with emeralds and sapphire glittering in the torchlight. The other, contains an orange powder, woven from spiced plants of hot and sweet tastes in the air. A divine smell erupts in the nostrils of every member of the court, but the whispers continue regardless of the pleasantries. Like dripping fangs of venomous predators.

Lord Henry stands and walks down to Joseph. He raises his hand into the air, palm out straight just above the Prince's eye level. "Blessed are our paths, friend of the Pathlands and follower of the ways. I give thanks to the gifts you bring to me and honor your welcome with open arms."

Joseph raises his head, smiling pearl white teeth towards Alayna's father.

"Now, let's eat, I'm starving!" Henry joyfully pats Joseph on the shoulder, wrapping his arm around him.

Joseph turns his head to Alayna, momentarily drops his smile, turning it into a quizzing stare, raising his eyebrows before beaming a smile directly at her.

Rosey cheeks come about her face, and with it, a flutter of wings in her stomach as her eyes cast themselves down to her feet, flicking her hair over her features like curtains. For a moment, Alayna felt taken off her feet, without even speaking to the man or knowing his intentions. Her mind is pierced with girlish thoughts as he turns to walk with her father. They exchange words as they walk, both stealing a few glances back at Alayna as they do, making her wonder what they are saying. The whispering voices excited by this development, audible – attention turned to familiarity between Henry and Joseph.

They arrive at the banquet table and Henry is greeted with warmth by the servers who hand him and Joseph the first two plates of silver from the stack in the age-old way that the host leads the commencement of the feast. The crowd follows his lead, already hungry with anticipation from the inviting sights and smells that emanated from the delights at the table. The whispering falls to a low hum.

The lids to the serving dishes are raised one by one by the servants who administer it, revealing fruits, pickled vegetables, turkey crowns, and roasted potatoes drizzled with honey and thyme. A fine spread and a fine occasion that many will speak of in years to come.

The Lord fingers some pieces and sets them about on his plate in an unorganized fashion as his legs maneuver themselves back towards the throne while he sneaks in one or two grapes that may have missed placement onto his array. There, he and Joseph begin to speak with one another, too distant an ear shot for Alayna.

"Blushing?" Her mother brushes her hand onto her hair.

Alayna, however, does not reply, but only stares at her feet. The butterflies in her stomach die before they can fly away.

"He's a handsome young man, I'll give you that. I wouldn't consider him a Prince though, he's only one of those imperial boys with stiff lips and no backbone and they also don't truly follow the eight paths, just some knock off unorthodox version."

Her speech quietens as she lowers down to Alayna's ear level, tucking her dress in under her feet, licking her poisonous lips.

"He isn't interested in you like that. I don't know why you're getting so invested. There are so many other people who are on your level of beauty and anyways, he might just want you for title and power." She glares and tilts her head and pauses shortly.

"Nothing more."

Alayna turns and looks her mother in the eyes, only to be greeted by a venomous grin with the tip of her tongue sticking out between her teeth. Her nails scratch against the hard oaken chair as they become more and more vigorous until her hand clenched into a fist. Her veins in her arm pop up as her glare turns into a snarl. Her mother slips back behind the throne, resting her chin against the top.

"Shut up." Loud enough for her mother to hear, but only a whistle to the glaring court. Alayna, fixed to the chair, hands deep and engraved into the wood, clenches her jaws and shakes ever so slightly with anger and frustration.

A hushed tone slips under Arabella's tongue and into Alayna's ears. "I'll remember that you silly little girl. No one speaks to me like that." She strides off, leaving Alayna to fester in her hatred, and Alayna's eyes dance away, vying for control over her anger and fear.

She stares over to her father. A man who has always given her his time, always provided her with refuge when he was around. He was laughing, chatting with his guests, eating, drinking, and enjoying himself. At least he was happy.

Whether or not she hated her mother, Alayna loved her father. She loved him with all her heart. He was a kind, gentle man with a soul so delicate that his subjects loved him too. But he had the iron will and strength of a warrior that he only showed to those who wronged him or his family.

Her father's eyes catch hers; they stare for a moment until he puts on a proud face of love and kindness. His body language implied he would come back over to her, but before he could even think about ending his conversation, Arrabella snatched him away out of sight. Like a wolf with a deer.

She becomes aware of steps slapping up against the stone floor of the seated platform, and a boy, maybe 16, cautiously makes his way up. He stops before the last step and bows with his head perpendicular to the stairway.

"My Lady." He sheepishly awaits her reply.

Alayna quickly pushes her hair back, allowing it to dangle behind her shoulders once more. "You may rise. What is your name?" Her words ring out like a wet rag, practiced only with Martha until now for the suitors that announced themselves to her after her father had left her side.

He lifts his head, brow to the floor, astounded by Alayna's beauty that now shows itself to him.

"My la, la, Lady…"

His words lose him, like wondering through a forest with no path or direction. Mesmerized by her hair, her eyes as if they were entwining him within the root.

"Yes, you have already said that…"

Stern. Like as if her mother was pulling the strings. They came out of her like a weeping wound. Uninvited but unstoppable.

The boy is large, his plump puppy fat hadn't gone away since he had grown up to adolescence, but yet he carried with him a teenage smell.

"Do forgive me… It's my first time…. You're absolutely…" He pauses, again lost for words.

"Absolutely what?" The puppet still plays Alayna's strings. But now she feels like she cannot stop herself. Like she likes it. Like she is copying the strings' movements herself.

"Beautiful, Lady."

Alayna smiles.

"My Lady, you mean?"

The boy does not respond.

"And what about your name and house?"

He stands still, catching the glares from behind him while the sweat drops off his brow.

"I'm Fennek of House Trevant…. Travant, I mean." He scratches his nose, hoping the world didn't hear his Freudian slip.

"That will do, Fennek. Thank you." She palms her hand in the air, gesturing for his retreat.

He bows, moving with a sidestep down the steps and into the crowd. The eyes of the court watch his every move. Like vultures to a passing lost man in the desert. At least they did not look at her, and if they did, they wouldn't see her as prey at this point anyway.

She stares at her trembling hands, her mind trying to loosen the strings. But they don't leave her, fastening like little nooses around her fingers and wrists. She pushes her body back gently against the chair, as another set of footsteps make their way up the stone steps.

She sighs.

"My Lady..." A male voice airs in the room again. A different one. Stabbing her ears, opening a healed wound.

Alayna takes a deep breath, trying to steady her nerves. She knows this is just the beginning. A long night of formalities and forced pleasantries lies ahead. But a flicker of excitement, a spark of something unexpected, stirs within her. Perhaps this choosing won't be as dreadful as she anticipated. After all, shes only sixteen once.

The evening was young, and suitors began to line up in the hall. All while the cawing of a raven bellows into the hall. An uninvited message.

9

Sir Osric Erenbell - Perceptions and Perspectives

A hasted step across the winter wood startles the scarce critter rummaging on the snowy floor. It bolts into the tree out of sight with no morsel of food to accompany its mouth. It goes hungry.

Osric's face sharpens as it stares at the snowy landscape. Little arches of woodland peppered with little puffs of smoke from chimneys as he sees the village in the distance. His ears cast to behind him as a twig snaps and footsteps dissipate behind the path of trees.

Osric's sword is drawn as he turns to face whatever follows him, but it is only a deer. A lonely doe that darts to safety. It's far too north to survive this climate. Far too north to live.

His sword props back into its sheath as he eyes the deer's path. It leaps to within just an eye shot then disappears into the distant fog.

Osric sighs, a breath of cold air snatches his exhalation and adds to the growing mists.

He follows it, as it floats with the wind, smothering the distant flutters of doe skips.

A sharp pain tears into his left shoulder. He looks down in pain as blood has splattered onto his chest piece. His blood. He sidesteps and makes his way to a tree as a whistling sound cuts next to his ear, missing his head by inches.

"Show yourself, you coward." Osric breaks the silence with his call, fumbling in his bag as his eyes look to the trees and to the white woodland's edge. He pulls out a small hand crossbow, no larger than a plate or bowl, and loads a barbed bolt with strong twine.

"Show yourself, now! State your business." No words meet his, only the rustling of the leaves from the cold winds. Osric peers behind a tree but darts back as a bolt is fired.

Osric grins, knowing the location of the shooter.

"Birch tree, on the left."

A sharp eye.

"You have five seconds to drop your weapon and show yourself or you will suffer the consequences."

The wind again, only the wind meets his call.

"Five..." Osric pauses and hears the rearming of a crossbow.

"Four..." Footsteps make their way out into the open.

"I am a knight of Xanathose, I order you to drop your weapons and surrender. Three!"

Osric peers the other side of the tree, and a bolt is again fired by a man in the open. It navigates through the woods and hits the bark embedding itself into the fleshy wood pulp.

Osric makes haste, his sword drawn in his right hand as he lifts his left to aim at the person reloading. A gasp as the shooter is unprepared for a direct assault and erupts into a wail, screaming as his bow is undrawn.

"No! Don't hurt me!"

The bolt fires and aims true, catching him in the leg between where the two muscles meet the tendon. He startles at first, letting out a squeal of pain as he falls back, leaving his leg to rest in place. The bolt lodged firmly within.

Osric tugs at the twine. "I'm going to give you the rest of your five seconds to explain who you are. Three."

A gulp of saliva to match the pain, as the cloaked figure unhoods, scratching at the snow-covered earth to try and hoist himself away.

"Woodbee. Woodbee Grange." A stale man, with freckled cheeks and damaged orange-like hair, stares distraught. Osric remembers and a realization falls on his face.

"The hunter." Osric tugs the string, snatching at the man's skin as the barbs try to pry loose but latch on to fresh flesh.

He lets out a groan.

"Yes. I'm only following orders, sir. Please." He pleads with his eyes. "Please sir."

Osric looks at the fear in his eyes and stares through him. "Who sent you?"

He holds his sword up now, threatening his main artery in his leg.

"The Baron. Sir, please let me live. I was only doing what he said."

"Why." He twists the twine, embedding it into his flesh, spluttering out flecks of blood as his face boils.

"He said, if you come out of the cave without the orcs head then I should shoot you. That be all my Lord. Please!"

Osric nods and then yanks the string from the huntsman's leg, letting out a cry of pain. The bolt dangles in the air, covered in blood and some blobs of flesh. Like a pendulum swinging with motion.

"Shoot at me again, and I'll aim for that stupid brain in your head. Understand?"

"Yes. Yes sir. Yes, my Lord."

He grovels to his feet and limps with vigor through the forest, gripping whatever tree or shrub he can, with eyes remaining fixed behind his shoulder.

Osric reels in his crossbow and puts it back into his bag. He looks up to the sky and exhales, letting out a breath of misty air. He remains there for a moment, just out of sight, but then follows the trail of blood-soaked footsteps in the snow with his eyes.

He looks at his sword that is charged with adrenaline, shaking in his hand as he sheathes it and then follows the trail back towards the village. Like breadcrumbs through a wood.

A while passes while the trail is fresh, more blood seems to show up the closer he gets to the village until he hears the grunting and shouting of the Baron and the pleading of Woodbee.

Osric steps into a thicket of bushes that brush the sides of the pig farm on the village edge and moves himself around to be within earshot.

"You bloody idiot. You let him get away?" Woodbee grovels, clinging to the Baron's legs.

"But my Lord. He's an anointed knight. He's the famous Sir Osric. How can I even dream of actually hitting him?"

The Baron's face squeezes and angers under his fat cheeks that shake with fury.

"So, you admit to not being up to the task? You admit to failure and admit that you took this on without truly knowing the difficulty of the mission?"

A few of the Baron's henchmen loiter around, armed with pikes, crossbows, and leather armor.

"No. I'm up to it! I'm up to it! I promise my lord."

Woodbee launches his head towards the Baron's thigh, pleading and weeping. Partly from the pain, partly from fear.

The Baron rests his jeweled fingers between Woodbee's hair, gently rubbing it. He looks to one of his henchmen and nods towards the hunter.

The henchman points the crossbow where the head meets the neck at the back and shoots point-blank, letting the bolt sink into his spine, leaving a snap.

Woodbee drops to the floor, paralyzed from the neck down, gasping for breath as the Baron grabs his hair again and looks him dead in the eyes. "Cowards don't go to the gods, you little shit. May you get lost on your walk across the paths and struggle as the forest takes you forever." He throws the hunter's body to the ground as the head bounces, leaving a puddle of blood.

"I want his head on a pike in the square and I also want you to gouge out his eyes so his body in the afterlife cannot find the way ahead." The henchmen nod fearfully, shuddering at the thought, all while following their orders.

Goodsberry turns to the townspeople who have gathered in bunches. "I will not tolerate cowardice in our homes and hearts. This man failed to bring Osric back to answer for his crimes. He ran like a bloody dog."

His voice raises slightly. "You are all good people. Brilliant people. The Greatest people in Caldaria. But I must call you all for aid in my time of need."

He repeats, holding his hand to his heart. "Our time of need."

"Tomorrow, I wish to march on this creature in force and ask that all able-bodied men take up arms and join me and my men in dispatching this evil from the land."

His words are greeted with a cheer from some townspeople.

"If we can bring Osric to justice, I would prefer that. He's a renowned man, a great man, but has been twisted by blight, that scourge that sours are farmland and kills our people."

Osric shakes his head in confusion, his eyes wide and intense, struggling to decipher the conversation. He sees Arelle dart into the Rookeries Rest tavern with her eyes looking at her back while the rally in the village square continues. A craze of mad men.

Osric carefully moves through the thicket, hugging the bushes so that he does not reveal himself, but listens out with his ears.

"Tomorrow, I will expect to see a crowd of men, with pitchforks and bows waiting in the square. That day will mark the end of this scourge as we break his bones and burn his flesh."

A cry of maniacal cheering bellows out from the village like an army of crazed fanatics. They parade through the streets towards the Baron's Hall and pile in like bees to a hive.

Out of sight, he looks around, as he exits the thicket and hides behind a hovel opposite the tavern. The streets are dead, with only the snow and ice to give company to the wood thatched buildings.

Osric bursts into the pub, similar to the first night, he first entered, only to be greeted by Arelle carrying a packed bag and a worried look on her face, now startled by his presence.

10

Martha Honoroa - The Wick to the Flame

A blood-soaked rag scratches against the sanguine-stained flooring outside the Great Hall. The cut-through indents of the slab absorb like a sponge and then harden like concrete. It's difficult to get out, staining the very stone it lies upon.

Morning licks the horizon, blushing at the clouds as it climbs up the sky. Many guests left in the early hours. As they open the doors, it lights up the stone slabs once more, making it easier to clean before closing again and being left in darkness.

Martha is tired, aching, but still humming her lullabies, without a stain of tears on her cheeks. Even though the very blood she cleanses is from another one of the girls she raised from a child. This is a common occurrence, and she has simply gotten used to it.

She lifts the rag and places it into the diluted, bloodied water held in a wooden bucket with an iron handle. The water rings out and flows like torrential rain, pouring Ezra out like dribble. Each ring of the rag is just another bitter farewell. The tapping of footsteps across the stone floor makes its way towards Martha.

She works with her head down, focusing on the last remains of blood that carve themselves out on the floor as she scratches with the rag. The footsteps draw closer, as a beguiling shadow begins to loom over her head, she can feel it.

"Nearly finished then. Taken you a while?" Arrabella's voice snaps, breaking the cold as the warmth of the sun beacons.

"Yes, my Lady, about eight hours. Blood has gone and soaked into the stone."

The rag scratches the slabs with vigor.

"Well, I trust your judgment. You deserve a break for the day."

Martha says nothing at first as her mind is fixed on the floor. She knows of Arrabella's games on the downtrodden and weak. "Thank You, my Lady."

Arrabella taps her face with her finger, pondering the sky, plotting a worthy punishment for Martha's existence.

"In the kitchens. I do fancy one of your exotics... Now what's the word?"

"Curry, My Lady."

She takes her finger from her face and wags it. "Yes! The one with mutton! It's lovely!"

Martha nods, placing her rag into the bucket and picking it up.

A smile races across Arrabella's face as it excretes hatred. "I think the party guests will enjoy a bowl of it tonight. We will need about 300 portions."

She twinkles her fingers. "I think we will need it by supper time and don't overcook it like last time, dear? I'll let Lord Henry know you're in charge of the pleasantries tonight. He will be most pleased."

Martha's hand grabs her back, and she lifts up to kneel before her. "Yes, my Lady."

Arrabella walks with a strut in her foot towards the hall. She opens the door and slips within its chambers.

79 years ago, Martha was born a Princess in the faraway Kingdom of Honoroa. She married well and had a good life, with fine dresses, jewelry, and the best of servants. She was pampered and treated those that served her well. She birthed a son and daughter and had many happy years. Until the war, when her husband was killed at the battle of the spice fields.

These were dark days for her kin, so many men died, not just hers, pawns in a game of religious chess that came about by questioning its authority. Her home was taken, and she was sent off to the Gesantians as a hostage and treated as a slave.

Her parents, son, and daughter fled north, escaping on boats from the royal docks, taking as many refugees as they could with them. She had high hopes they would make it through, being guided by some of the best bodyguards to ever grace Caldaria. But she hasn't heard from them since. They come to her in her dreams, laughing, loving, playing, but sometimes those dreams are under a veil of nightmares. Maybe they are alive. Her parents would have passed by now. Her son and daughter, she hopes, are well, happy, and at peace. Maybe she will meet them one day, whether that's in this life, or, on the Walk to the Well Wood, taking the right road on the crossroads in the afterlife.

Her old country now rests as a dowry to the Prince of Gesantia, the baby killer Prince Corvus, until the day of her death. The Gesantians forced marriage upon Martha when Corvus was merely months old, binding it in magic to sow it into the fabric of this world.

It means that when she dies of old age, Martha's titles and birthright will pass to her husband, meaning Gesantia will rule two Kingdoms, not only by claim, but by magical contract.

Something that cannot be broken unless you bring cataclysm upon the world.

She is here until that day, bound by an oath sown into the very magical fabrics of the world that bind everything together. If she does not die of old age, then a turning of events will most indeed occur, like they have done before. You cannot break the bindings of Caldaria without the weight of the world crashing against you and the world around it. And by the gods, you will hope for a quick death.

Some stories tell of fire burning from the sky, destroying cities and towns. Others of plagues that ravaged for tens of years. The elves used to call this magic the forging and entwining. Only elves can cast magic like that without an elf tear, and they have been gone for over 200 years.

Martha walks through the kitchens, with maids and servants busy cleaning last night's pots and silverware, ready for this evening's banquet. As she walks by, they all greet her like soldiers to a respected general. She waves at them, sharing hugs and shoulder pats until she gets to the cookery room where two chefs stand next to a pot.

"Morning Marfa, how be you?"

A big green orc, standing eight feet tall, dons a chef gown and large ladle, dipping it into a large cauldron bubbling away a large pot of boiled oats in milk.

Martha nods a respectful courtesy and smiles. "I'm good, Chef, you get out of bed alright this morning?"

He scratches his long nose and leaves a big cheesy grin between his tusks. "Nah, had too much ale with this one last night. Knows how to drink e' does. Ended up getting up just before that rooster called."

A little gnome with a ginger beard blossoms from his chins. Rosey cheeks standing on top of a stool as he sprinkles in some cinnamon. "Morning Martha." He smiles.

"Morning, Pocket. Now, gents, I must go and pick up some bits from the market in town. Our beloved Lady wants some of that mutton curry, and I'm not sure if we have any chili."

She pauses for a moment. "Have we got any mutton, or do we need that too?"

Chef scratches his chin. "I fink we have both, Mumma M. No need for the trip. If you head down inta the larda, you should find what you're looking for in the barrel with the knot on the lid."

She smiles. "Saves me a trip. Thanks, boys. I'll get the bits and we can start."

Pocket steps from the stool and climbs up the chef's trousers and then onto his shoulder as he reaches for a plump bunch of gooseberries that dangle from the height of the ceiling pane. He throws one or two into the porridge oats and yams in another to his mouth. He then climbs down and begins to stir using a spoon larger than him.

Martha takes each step carefully as each creak on the steps weakens the already warped wood. She makes her last step off the bottom, holding her lower back, adjusting her aching hips.

The larder was full, mostly of exotic fruits and vegetables ready for the remaining banqueting days. Some carried smells of sweet scents that litter the nose and moisten the tongue while others carry peppery satisfaction that lurks like a haze over all of the food. Little fish hang from racks on the ceiling, scraped with flakes of salt and garnished with dill.

She steps, taking in great breaths of refreshing smells as she moves through the larder to the barrels at the back. Each lid, labelled unpleasantly with little orcish symbols like graffiti on a wall.

But then, there staring her in the face was the lid with the knot. That wasn't what caught her attention though, her eyes seemed to catch something else behind all of the barrel's. A hole in the wall, no bigger a space for someone to crawl through, had been hidden badly behind the scattered wooden containers.

Oddly, Martha hadn't seen this before, it sparked some confusion, but at the same time, she paused her thoughts. If Arrabella found out about the hole, heads would roll, and she would see her loved ones die and then be replaced.

"Mumma M, you ain't fallen down der ave ye?" A loud, brutish wail ricochets down the stairs.

Martha steadies her body, lifting her chest into the air. "No, but can you both please come down here."

A mumble rumbles from upstairs, and a few thuds as Chef almost charges down the stairs, missing steps in his descent. Martha looks at him but points at the hole.

"Rats? Or do we have a worse problem?"

Chef scratches his brow and snuffs with his nose. "Dont smell like rats mumma, rats smell stinky."

Martha looks intrigued but mostly perplexed.

"Then lets cover this hole for now and fill it once the party has finished."

11

Saracen Murdock - The Needle and the Thread

Saracen awakes with a head full of sweat as he unravels the memories from the nightmares squeezing out the sanity from him like a bloody rag.

His eyes open now, clear and adjusting to the low light of the sheltered morning dew. The roof is made of thatch, entwined with ivy and grape vines that droop like hands to grab the building's supports.

He shudders at first, letting his arms crack and stretch. He feels no feeling in his left. A bandaged stump over his elbow is all that is left of his wound, well sown and doused in healing herbs and the smell of liquor still perfumes its twine. His nose is itchy, and chest is slightly tight.

He does not sweat or ponder any longer, but sighs as clarity between dream and reality stares back at him. His head falls back down onto the straw mattress. He has lost his left forearm completely. Reality sinks in even harder, as the realization that the sadistic rebel has severed it and rubbed it into the mud so he would die a slow death.

Only then does he start to question his whereabouts. Is he dead? Who has dealt with his wound so skilfully? Is this the beginning of the long road to the crossroads? A passing of one's soul into the eternal walk only to join your family and friends or to be lost and become one of the pathless. Is this the start of a journey? Will he see his father and mother again? Is his Father alone?

He sits up and yawns to the ceiling as his eyes let loose on his surroundings. The hut is small, with twigs and roots that make up the floor. Books adorn the shelves that corner the room, with healing symbols on stems and candles with half burnt wicks that sit as dividers. The smell is of lavender and ash, but more of a sickly smell that spirits its way into Saracen's nostrils which poltergeist uninvitedly in.

"Are you feeling any better?" A call rummages its way through one of the open windows. It is sweet, motherly and soft, swarming through the air like a wisp.

"Who are you?" Saracen follows the words but finds no figure.

"I found you, screaming in the night, cold and alone on the battlefield. I could put you back if you prefer?"

A cold shudder catches Saracen's guard as it etches its way through his spine wriggling his nerves.

"The crows had already made a meal on your arm before I could get it back. You're lucky to be alive. You're lucky to be able to stand."

Saracen rests his feet on the floor, putting little pressure on his painful legs.

"Thank you." His words shelter beneath his curiosity. "What is your name?"

A young woman with fiery ginger hair enters through the door, closing it behind her. Her hair curls and hugs her head hiding her collar bone and ears.

"Tyria."

A calm voice supports the air and sweetens the smells in the room as the candle wicks sparkle and flame begins to burn. She casts a smile, holding a walking stick and wheezing ever so slightly as she now scampers forward.

It is a surreal setting, a perfect little room in a homely dwelling with a beautiful hostess. If only for her deportation, would he think he is on the walk to the Well Wood.

"Ma.. Magic?" Saracen's eyes flicker between her and the now blue flame that burns a hue into the room. She balances each step onto her stick, unable to move her right leg at all, dragging it like a loose appendage sitting at the end of the bed facing him with her beauty.

"Yes." Her eyes ponder, almost like they float away as she looks to the ceiling letting her eyes become slightly paler. "Magic. That's what the other races like to call it."

She raises her hand and flicks her fingers in the air like a conductor would instruct their orchestra. A spiral of smoke flushes from her eyes, like a curtain rail dropping its cloth, smothering the air and expiring into no more than a ball.

Her eyes go a pale milky white, almost covered with a layer of haze as she stares into the distance.

"Magic can't cure people who use magic, I've been blind all my life. But sometimes people are surprised when miracles happen like the gods make their way into our lives suddenly, giving out their power for free."

Her hand closes, and the magic dissipates between her fingers and into the air around it like pipe smoke does after exhalation.

"Magic is an illusion, a mystery, a gift. Elves have been able to harness it for thousands of years. It is the very power that brought Caldaria to its knees, and the very power that built the foundations you all exploit now long after my kin left this world."

She stands, treading barefoot on twigs and roots towards the open window. "But now we are all gone, gone from this world and to never return."

Saracen stares towards the window, joining where her essence cries out too with his own eyes.

"Where did they go?" He hides his words like a rogue does his dagger. Concealed behind a cloak of abashment.

Tyria sighs. "I don't know. I'm stuck here with you all. Staring into the abyss waiting for an answer."

Her essence no longer sways towards the window, and she lets her head fall into her neck. Her tone is one of loneliness, defeat and bitterness.

"They left me here, 200 years ago they all left without a word or a thought or a whisper. I was alone for so long. No one to care for or that cared for me. No one to talk to. No one to love or that loved me."

A painful flow of words is forced out of her mouth as her throat swells up like a reaction to a bee sting.

Saracen does not dare to confront it more, nor continue the conversation; its stale end is more than enough but it merely only opened up more questions.

"And who do you fight for then?"

A slow pause falls across the room after she breaks the silence with this question that usually only a human would mutter. Maybe she is trying to connect with him.

"Gesantia? Or the rebels?"

Tyria's presence turns towards Saracen, awaiting a palatable response.

"My Queen, I fight for Gesantia and my Queen."

He lifts himself up, gaining balance from the mattress and looks around frantically. "Where are my things? My weapons? My armour?"

Tyria frowns and stares towards him. "Your possessions? Oh, my sweet boy."

Her eyes look dead into his. "The man who nearly killed you took your sword and then, when you passed out, the Lord and his men stripped you of all your armour, weapons and finery leaving you with nothing but the clothes you're in now as they tossed you into the piles of dead."

He looked down to his feet.

"Yes, they even took your boots," she says. "Don't you see Saracen Murdock."

His eyes flash back to hers, staring at her with boiling blood. "How do you know my name?"

It isn't anger that trifles with his emotions, more agitation. A fearful spark that shocked his very being.

"The path you have chosen has carved your fate in stone. You cannot run from it now."

His blood begins to simmer as he stares back at her with curiosity like before.

"How do you know my name? I need to know."

She reaches for his hand, and he receives it fearfully.

"You've known all your life that this wasn't it for you. That's why you joined the army. You left your quiet little town behind, your father, your friends and ventured out to see the world."

She pauses.

"This journey you are about to embark on, has no real ending, or cure, or outcome. Only the people will decide that. You will be one of the many to stand in defiance from a world which could engulf all worlds into darkness."

She looks at him with a sense of urgency. "But that is still not going to be enough."

His anger bubbles over again and boils his blood like a hot kettle on a fire. "How do you know my fucking name."

His hand pushes against the air and the candles all flicker out.

He stops and gasps and Tyria smiles.

"Along the road you seek, a pathway you will take along the crossroads of life. You will meet many who are crying for help, ones who will need you to save them from an early end in this world. But there will be one you will find on the long road, at the end of Gesantia and at its last hope. A child will cry for help, without a mother or a father to guide it. And you will save that child so that they can achieve their destiny in this world."

She pauses and looks at him with a fury in her eyes as her hair begins to burn like a red flame, torching her clothes in a white glow.

"For if you fail Saracen, let it be known..."

Her eyes begin to glow a sickly blue light, as the flicker of the candlewicks erupt in a chaotic fashion as the wax of each candle bubbles faster and faster.

"All realms will burn and the shadow that lurks beneath our feet will bring a new age. One that we will not be a part of."

Her fingers snap and a flourish of air begins to build, shaking the floor, walls, and roof. The energy builds, the shaking crescendos break the house apart, and pick up the pieces into a whirlwind crescendo before stopping abruptly. Twigs, rock, and clumps of mud fall at speed, crashing into the ground. Nothing is left standing.

The dust agitates his sensitive eyes, still adjusting to light and sight. He shields them with his hand, relieved to feel the light smattering of drizzle that will dampen the dust quickly. His nostrils are burning, and his lungs feel uneasy. A minute passes, he unshields his eyes and there, lying on the floor, is a skeletal carcass holding a walking stick.

A chill runs down his spine and this time it hollows over him like grim shadows. As if the trees of the forest around him loom over his shoulders like spies watching his every breath. There, within the forest, is the beating magic of a Well Wood tree. Its white bark flows a blue trickle that rolls into the ground as its roots tear through the environment around it.

He stands, bare feet smothering with a mud that wriggles around his toes. His mind, hazed and confused with burning questions. But before attempting to find their answers, there is one answer he seeks more than anything else.

12

Lady Alayna Astravix - He Loves me, He Loves me Not

Alayna sits up exhausted from her resting eyes. It is the morning after meeting the suitors and her mouth remains painful after her fake smiles and from making small talk from the previous day.

The light of day is only moments from appearing but, alas, she has a knock on her door. A knock that she knows to be her father's.

She stretches her arms into the air, gets up out of bed and opens the door revealing a troubled man, a feeling that is painted all over his face.

"Father, what is it?"

Alayna sits in her chambers, unpinning her hair while her father sits on her linen and reads through a letter delivered in the early hours of the morning.

A broken red wax seal of the Gesantian tower braces against the torn parchment of an opened letter. It is addressed directly to Lord Henry Astravix. Henry clears his throat before reading aloud. "The rebels have destroyed the Queen's army and have laid siege to the capital."

He tosses the letter to the corner table and puts his head in his hands. "Her majesty is calling upon all outlying houses and their banners to meet them in the field regardless of any duty they are undertaking."

Alayna looks from the mirror towards her father. His eyes now look at her reflection with a fear that she has never seen in him before.

"You're not going? Are you? You can send Cousin Edward? You're far too old to be fighting now, father? Please." Her eyes well up, as she runs towards him throwing herself against his feet, scratching at his clothes and yanking at his arm.

"I have to go, Alayna. I am honor-bound, and it is my duty as a Lord of Gesantia." He stands, ignoring his daughter's cry as she falls back onto her bed in heaps.

"When will you go? Not now? It's my choosing day. I need you?"

His hand rests upon the door, opening it ajar as he looks down to the floor.

"Listen to me." His eyes glare back to her with failure in his breath while his hands brace against her shoulders. "One day, you will rule with your spouse over a castle or maybe even a kingdom. And on that day, you will look back to now and remember the day I had to go to war. The day I had to leave you here."

His words catch his tongue, stringing it up and tying the noose. "You will understand then. And maybe then, you will forgive me."

Her eyes now burn, while they fill with tears. "Father. I need you."

The door opens, with a defeated man standing in the arch. He looks down at his daughter, and his eyes beg forgiveness, forgiveness for leaving her on this special day - something no father would ever want to do to their daughter. But no words leave his mouth, as a grim hateful look comes across his face as he steps out of the room. A face angry at the world.

The door closes, leaving Alayna scared and howling to the wind. It bellows out from her, crackling out her throat, tearing her voice box almost breaking blood. She stands, rushing through the door after her father but the floor is like mud, clinging to her legs as she cannot hasten fast enough. He is gone. Not even turning around to see her.

The cry turns silent, thrashing out empty beckons that filter into nothingness.

"Flower? What's wrong?" Martha waddles through the hallway towards her, carrying folded linen in her left hand.

Alayna still cries, holding onto the red-carpet clinging to it like a duvet. Her eyes catch Martha, and she grasps to her leg for comfort, clawing at her sewn garments and weeping.

"Come, come. I'll make you some of my special herbal tea, the one my mother used to make for me, and we can talk." Martha holds Alayna's shoulder lifting her with whatever strength she can muster and walks her into the room. She falls onto her bed, balling into a heap and clenching into a ball.

"Flower. What's up?" Concern strikes across Martha's face, battling against Alayna's will.

"He's gone. He's gone." Alayna stares blankly, filling the void with thought.

Martha opens her mouth, but before the words come out of her a bell sounds from the castle chapel, it rings and chimes once. Then twice. Then three times. It is a sign that the Lord of the castle has left his manor. Martha then twigs and begins to realize what is going on.

"Flower? Shall we go see him off? Maybe it's what he would want. Maybe it will make you feel better?"

Alayna stands, hobbling to her feet, almost mirroring Martha's step. Words do not want to leave her mouth, and yet she trudges through what feels to be meadows of mud that varnish the floor.

She nods, looking at Martha with eyes that fill with anguish, scarred by many weeks of pain and tears.

She steadies herself and finds her feet once more, grabbing Martha's rough hand and holding it deeply, pulling herself close like very dear friends. They walk hand in hand to the top of the tower, Martha climbing each step with heavy breath guiding Alayna's, whose eyes are drenched full of tears while Alayna unknowingly helps Martha by being her grounded weight up the steps for her frail back.

The wind greets them first, then a drizzle of rain that begins to hide Alayna's sorrow that now flows freely again from her eyes. There, in the distance, is a troop of men marching with haste into the distance, carrying the standard of house Astravix.

Lightning cascades across the landscape of forest and crag followed by the scream of thunder which charges its partnered lightning bolt with fear and entropy. Martha pulls Alayna closer, letting most of the rain fall atop of her rather than on the girl she has nursed, comforted and cared for like a daughter... Her fingers run through her hair.

"Oh, sweet child, we head to the old world. Back up straight and shoes tied tight.

Oh, sweet child we head to the old world. Light your torches and stay out the night."

Alayna's nerves calm, as the lullaby meets her ears.

"I've had some time to think about what you said. About coming with you when you go." Martha's hand strokes her head letting flicks of hair fall to her shoulders and tucking other locks behind her ear. "As long as you pick someone from Gesantia, I'll come with you."

Alayna's ears pipe up listening to one soft tune and now this. Her arms squeeze tighter holding her close, but her thoughts loosen as she remembers the man who entered the halls last night. Joseph. He was not a Gesantian, but from a country far to the south.

"Thank you, Mumma M. What will mother say?"

Martha continues to stroke her head.

"When the war is over, write to the Queen. Explain where you are going and request for me to come with you. She won't care, as long as I am in her kingdom."

Martha's eyes begin to soften, leaving tears to fall atop of Alayna's head. Within all this dread and terror, two hearts beat atop a tall tower, enjoying each other's company in a dark world. A flicker of light sparkles in Martha's eye, glittering her tear drop as it falls.

The morning dew combats the horizon as the dark clouds begin to cease. As the sun comes up, the flags stand to attention against the wind, singing colors that would make a rainbow blush.

Gesantia hasn't sent all their forces to aid the capital, those chosen to remain ready themselves wearing ceremonial attire, glad to be bone dry and at the castle feast. The kitchens and serving staff, are rushed off their feet attending to guests residing within and preparing for another day's festivities.

A parade of flags enters the courtyard and horns trumpet to sound a wakeup call to all those who have overslept after the nights partying.

"Alayna. listen to me." Martha's hands grab her shoulders, pushing her to an arm's distance and looking in her eyes. "I know this is hard for you. It is like your own battle. Fight the war you must face and be strong. He needs that from you now."

Alayna musters her courage, moving her head up enough to be in eye contact with Martha's eyes. "I had better get dressed."

Alayna walks towards the stairwell and stops, looking back at a frail old lady staring back at her. Her worn skin, and crooked back are overlooked as the sun shines from behind her head.

"Thanks, Mumma M."

Even during these unpredictable times, they both share a smile with each other before returning to the games of life.

13

Sir Osric Erenbell - The Honourable Rogue

The pit still bubbles a broth, cackling as it spews out hot, beautiful scents, but the fire has long since burned out.

The hall begins to feel the weight of the cold from the outside pushing against the thatched roof and into the bones of both Arelle and Osric. Osric rearranges himself as he pushes the door to a close behind him, with Arelle gasping at his sight.

"Sir Osric? My father. My father is looking for you," she says nervously, as she creeps around the table. Her eyes gaze to and from Osric's eyes and his sheathed blade.

Osric looks over concerned and slightly confused as his face frowns.

"You're the Baron's Daughter? But you work in the tavern?"

She moves forward. "I know." Her eyes flicker to the floor momentarily before looking back towards him, which quizzes her.

Osric takes his sword from his belt sheath and places it atop the table, all while taking a seat. He fashions his steel bracers that are clamped around his arms, allowing comfort.

"My father sent a man to kill you," Arelle's words pain her as she says them. They are stained by a grim grotesqueness that hides behind her eyes.

"I begged him to use reason. I begged him. But all he kept repeating was that you were brainwashed by the monster? That the monster somehow got into your head?"

He raises his hands up above the table, clear and visible. "I was there to kill a monster. But I found no monsters. Only a scared orc looking for his wife. Nothing more."

Osric stands, watching Arelle's hands roll against the table as she maneuvers herself to safety. "What would you do if you had everything taken away from you, Arelle? What would you do if your family were put in harm's way?"

His fist clenches against the table as he looks to his feet, letting out a pitted sigh before looking back to her face.

"Your father is a power-hungry man looking to plunge the north back into a racist and intrusive way, and I cannot have that." Osric stands, towering the room as a fury sparks in his eyes.

"I need to send a Raven to Xanathose before this situation gets out of hand." His words spit from his mouth like daggers, her eyes gently flicker towards the sword on the table and then back to him.

"Head upstairs then. The room to the right."

Arelle watches the man as his legs follow his eyes towards the stairs, making their way around the table. She seizes the opportunity and grabs the sword, unsheathing it and clumsily aiming it towards him with both hands struggling against the weight.

"Stop, I'm not afraid to hurt you." she says.

Osric's feet stand still as he raises his arms above his head and turns his body slowly towards her.

"Listen to me."

Arelle steps towards him, pointing the sword to his throat. "No, you listen to me. You're under a spell. The monster wanted you to kill people. My dad said so."

He sighs, lifting his eyes towards hers. "He's a liar, Arelle. You know it in your heart."

Struggling to hold the sword, she flings it up above her shoulder, using what little might she possesses, readying to swing it.

"You're the Liar!"

Bursting through the door is one of the Baron's men, adorning a tabard of a broken tower. He grasps a short sword in his hand and wears a bucket helmet. His eyes look at Arelle, and then towards Osric before he charges at him, preparing to lunge for his stomach.

Arelle's eyes turn and almost without thinking swings the sword to the Baron's henchman and cleaves the top of his skull, revealing a brain kept in an open shell.

His eyes flicker and peer around the room before falling lifelessly as the contents of his veins begin to pour out onto the wooden floor. It leaks through the floorboards, and drips can already be heard between the short silence that followed.

The sword falls from Arelle's hand as her blood-stained face falls with it, collapsing into a sense of misery. It clunks against the floor, bouncing against the crimson stains and splashing up against both of their feet.

She stares at him as small twitches of movement from his body begin to go limp, revealing a lifeless corpse. Hyperventilating and beginning to pant as she looks towards Osric, falling to her knees.

He runs towards her, catching her before she does and covering her mouth before she screams.

Holding her there for a while as she rocks back and forth.

"Arelle, listen to me. You need to snap out of this quickly before more come, okay?" He grips her tightly. "You need to be quiet while I send this raven. Can you do that?"

She stops her panting and nods as he lets go of her mouth. Osric stands over her, as she continues staring towards the dead man, still twitching muscular movement. He lifts his arms from her shoulders and stands over her like a shadow, all while taking those first steps back.

He jolts up the stairs, skipping a step with each movement he makes to reach the top and enters the room she suggested. He scrawls down a note on parchment and rams it into the raven's claws before releasing it through an open window. There was no time for a wax print or seal; that would have taken far too long to do.

He speeds his way back towards the landing and then back down towards Arelle who now clenches onto his blade again. Her arms barely lift it above her waist as she points it again towards him.

"I don't want to do that again."

She coughs, breaking a few tears now that have boiled into anger.

"I don't expect you to either." He holds his hand out. "Come with me. I'll keep you safe."

She lifts the blade forward in retaliation to his words as her mouth trembles with fear.

"I'm not going anywhere near you; how can I trust you? How can I trust anyone anymore?"

Osric looks on and watches as she begins to lower her arms.

"He hasn't been the same for a while, Osric. Something has changed about him, ever since he went on that hunting trip near Xanathose."

She lowers the blade slightly, partly because of the weight.

"My father came back atop a wagon, ready to be buried when they thought he had been killed in an ambush, but he woke up screaming in the night. Surgeons did what they could, and he survived..."

She pauses, looking Osric directly in the eye while her eyes visibly fill with tears.

"After that day, he started being sick, confining himself to his quarters, not acknowledging the death of my mother who died from a fever shortly after he left for the hunt."

She looks down to the floor, dropping Osric's blade with it.

"He was a loving man, one who loved his people and treated them with kindness no matter what race they were. Since his return, he has grown a cruelty within his heart. An obsession that changed him in every way that mattered, in every way that mattered to me."

She looks at him with a grim under her eyes and shudders as she kicks the blade back to him, struggling under its weight. He takes it and picks up the sheath which sits in a pool of the henchman's blood and places it on his belt.

"A while passed, and he started buying up all the houses and lands around the area and then made me the tavern maid of this inn.... I was glad of the company... I never see him anymore."

She stops, looking down to her shoes which are now stained with a thick gloop of blood and human brain.

Arelle turns, and without speaking, grabs Osric by the arm. Then says, "Promise me you won't kill my father." Her eyes were determined by his answer. They wished for it in every thought.

"You have my word."

Her grip claws against his arm, and with piercing eyes, she stares into his eyes. "Swear it by the Gods."

Osric returns her intense gaze, feeling the strength of her emotion through her stare and within her clasp around him. "I swear it."

A pause, delicate as if alone at night and a floorboard was to creak. Osric could tell she was at a knife's edge, confused and heartbroken about her father, but she was not at the point of no return yet. She had a long way ahead of her that he saw from the elf tear the first night they met, a hard journey, one filled with death, but overwhelmingly, one of happiness. An aspect of himself mirrored with her, like an old friend or relative. Seeing something in Arelle that he thought he lost all those years ago.

"Come on, let's get out of here before more of his men come."

She agrees hesitantly and they begin packing their bags with dried foods and make their way to the door, peering into the snowy landscape that fogs the trees and buildings outside. Arelle peers back at the corpse once more and with eyes closed prays for his safe passage along the paths. For sometimes, even the most corrupt of acts are forced by the puppeteer pulling the strings.

14

Lady Alayna Astravix - Plays from the past

A cheer brandishes against the crackling flags, and gleaming heat shines on the tourney and guests. It's a good day for the games.

Chivalrous knights adorn multi-colored flags and fine woven tabards, lining up before the audience, ready for today's games. Men and women in armor stand, fortunate in clad steel, carrying their weapons and shields proudly bearing the mark of their house and countries. They line up in front of honored guests, staring out towards Alayna and Arrabella, awaiting their confirmation on today's tournament.

Arrabella stands, with a delicate grin across her face and a determination in her breath.

"Good morning, everyone, and welcome to Day 2 of Alayna's choosing ceremony. I hope you all slept well!"

A round of applause sounds around the crowd, and the clanking of metal is heard from the knights who line the field.

"Today, we not only celebrate the ceremony but also celebrate Gesantian customs and the duty to uphold our laws and traditions. That is why, even though a war rages against our country, only my husband and his banners are called, and all of you are invited to stay, as it is written in law."

She pauses, awaiting the second applause to sound around the tourney ground, sounding louder and more vibrant than the first.

"We also thoroughly appreciate those who have volunteered to fight against our enemies, even though you are strangers to these lands. We salute those who took off this morning but applaud those who stayed to celebrate tradition."

A third round follows, and eyes peer towards Arrabella, who is lapping up the attention as she so usually does.

"Today marks the day of swords, a clashing of cultures and virtues. That is why today, our knights will be putting on a show, reminiscing about an old battle that took place against many of our families a long time ago in Honoroa. Today we celebrate our victory and annexation of their lands."

Cheers and applause sing out from the crowd, and a flurry of little banners are raised within the audience. A vast array of colors with banners from each house mixes up across the vast spectator area…

"Knights, the best combatant in this fight will obtain a reward of honor and a personal invitation to Alayna's wedding."

Following on from that comes a cheer, as the crowd chants their favorite knights on like celebrities. But the men and women in armor know that the prize is far greater than has been let on.

A fancily dressed man, with a red robe and fur-lined, pointed suede-like boots and buttoned trousers, rolls out from the crowd, lifting his arms into the air. "Let us hear it for Lady Arrabella!"

A roar is summoned from the audience, and they begin to chant "Edmond! Edmond!"

"So, today marks the day of virtues, a clashing of swords. For that reason, let me tell you a story!"

The crowd cheers as Edmond standing atop the fencing that separates the crowd from the tourney field. He carefully balances himself before walking the hammered wooden panels.

"Thirty-two years ago, men and women of our great nations fought a battle that has seen Gesantia, Inoria, West Watch, The Republic of Xanathose, and many more, stand in defiance of the traitors to The Paths at Honoroa."

The crowd is silent, like children waiting for their bedtime story, mesmerized by the presenter's narration and theatrical cheer. Arrabella sits overlooking the stairs to the honored seating area and watches as Martha struggles up them. Her glare is that akin to a panther.

"My Lady, you called?"

Arrabella gives a delayed smile and then pats an empty chair next to her and Alayna. "Yes, my dear, come sit, watch. Have the day off."

Martha bows, hesitantly looking towards the presenter who is perplexing the crowd with his story. She sits, laying her hands into her lap, nervously looking over to Alayna who watches Edmond with a smile.

Arrabella looks at her, grinning maniacally before sipping a goblet of wine and staring into the tourney field. Alayna rubs Martha's leg and smiles before looking at the tourney too.

"And so, when the royal family of Honoroa denounced the high clergy at Xanathose, renouncing all their ties to the one true religion and swearing fealty to heretical nonsense, what did we say?"

The crowd, baffled by the question, spurts out little huffs and chatters amongst themselves.

"We said, enough is enough! Xanathose declared a crusade, and TODAY! We will watch to see how this battle unfolded by using our knights to re-enact that event. Yes, today, right here, in this very tourney ground."

Alayna looks to Martha, who now looks stone-faced towards the grass. It is as if she has seen a ghost. Arrabella daintily swirls her wine goblet in her hand as she sits cross-legged with an insane, delighted grin across her face.

"Now let us give our combatants a cheer that even the gods may hear!" A thunderous applause awakens the intensity of the crowd, firing up the adrenaline of every knight who now lines up in a queue, one behind the other behind Edmond.

"Knights! Take a bead! If you choose blue, you fight for The Pathlands and should make your way to the blue flag! But if you choose red! You are a traitor and a heretic today! You fight for Honoroa!"

One by one, each knight puts their hand into the bag, revealing a color and moving to their respective spot, all until the last member puts their hand in the bag. They pull it out and reveal a blue stone, similar to their tabard colors that adorn their chest plate.

They look towards Alayna, and to Arrabella, and then finally Martha.

"Blue! Well done, sir!"

The knight hands the stone back, continuing the stare at Martha before making his way towards the blue team.

"And so, it was the year 2168, and our brave Crusaders made their way over sea, over land, over mountain and rock, before arriving at the gates of the capital city.

There, a horde of Honorites assembled in their thousands, meeting us outside in the spice field.

Oh, the day smelled of mirth of exoticness and rumbled the stomachs of many. But not everyone would come home that day!"

Turning his head away from the crowd, Edmond now looks towards the knights in armor.

"Knights! If both feet lift off the floor and you end up on your arse…" He pauses, preparing his finger, pointing it towards the Honorites. "…You're out!"

The finger follows the field and points towards the Pathlandians. From behind the presenter, the crowd cheers and claps.

The knights settle into formation, two columns of ten on either side, drawing their swords, axes, and mace.

"Trumpets!"

A sound cheers from the crowd as both battalions advance at each other, clashing their weapons against their shields.

"Ladies and gentlemen! I give you the Battle of the spice fields!"

Edmond jumps from the wooden panel and faces the field as columns from each battalion smash into each other locking horns like male mountain goats sparring for control. Steel crashes against steel, but yet no orders were barked among ranks, only a vying for control or satisfaction. Each knight wanting their share of the prize, that favour from the lord of the castle. For a heart-stopping moment, it seemed Honoroa might shatter the Pathlands' line. A surge of momentum pushed them forward, a wave threatening to break the dam. Then the knight in the blue tabard, bearing a large bastard sword and shield, breaks through the enemy formation like a charging rhino. He slams his shield into the back of one of the interlocked knights and then grabs hold of their adjacent ally by their steel backplate, slamming each of them together by the helmet before watching them fall backwards.

The commotion causes the Honorites to become completely surrounded, and almost within a few seconds, the knights representing the Pathlands win, putting most of the Honorites to the ground, having broken into their ranks.

A cheer screams from the crowd as even Arrabella herself stands to clap, releasing her hand from her wine goblet which sits on a side table to her right.

Edmond screams, running into the field and grasping the knight with the blue tabard's arm and raising it into the air. A calm passes amongst the crowd as they watch Arrabella gesture her hands.

"Dear sir knight, I think it is fair to suggest you were the fairest fighter in the field today. Without you, it's possible we may have had a different victor!"

The knight doesn't answer. He lowers his arm, while his head is still focused towards the pulpit.

"Sir knight, show us your face and tell us your name?"

The knight looks to the crowd and then bends his knee. He lowers his head and begins to remove his steel helmet.

"My name..."

He lifts his head, revealing an older man, no younger than forty, with dark skin and short curled hair. His face is scarred across his left eye, and the pigmentation of his skin is a lightish pink, possibly caused by a burn wound.

Martha sits uneasy, staring onwards towards him, almost like she has seen a ghost.

"My name is Jezel Honoroa, Prince and third in line to the throne of my homeland that was stolen from me."

Alayna snaps her head towards Martha and watches as she begins to stand out of her chair and begins to fall to her knees, groveling at the sight of him.

"No!"

Jezel looks to Martha, with a scarred face and clawed eyes, all before looking back to Arrabella with a fiery complexion.

Arrabella drops her goblet to the ground and pushes Martha out of the way and prone to the floor as she points towards him. Her face is wreaking putridly of sadistic tendencies, oozing a vile hatred. “Seize that heretic now!”

15

Saracen Murdock - Destiny never dies

Nightfall closes in around the forest as the prairie hides amongst their burrow and the firefly lifts its wings to give flight. Hooting owls and evergreen scents enrich the senses as the trickle of water adds to the ambience from a nearby stream.

The light of a distant Well Wood tree, shining brighter than the moon, lights the well-trodden dirt path, beguiling the beauty around it. It shrouds the forest in a sickly pale white, and chokes the trees and foliage, barely giving away the silhouettes.

Since his departure from Tyria's hut, Saracen has been wandering alone through the country, along the cobbled road and then towards the well-trodden path he is on now. Luckily, during his training, he was taught ways to hunt using items from the forest, and he knows what foliage and berries are safe to eat.

Saracen's eyes grow weary as he sees the smoke rising from a nearby village, one that he looks at with déjà vu. As a child, he played with his friends here, shaping leaves into boats to flow down the brook, making sure to be home before the Well Wood tree shone through the dark, piercing through the canopy above.

It is the village he grew up in, where many memories are made and flood his mind with childhood feelings. He stands at the forked road, before the blacksmith that hugs the village's outskirts. The tall forge lies cold, with scattered charred debris and numerous fallen, charred weapons that litter the floor.

Saracen looks uninterested, looking beyond the building and into the village. Further within, he sees doors blown off hinges and bodies that seem to have been thrown or cast out from their homes as men, women, and children lie lifeless, face down on the forest floor with no weapon or defense in their hands.

He still walks on, with little to no thought or remorse for those that lie there and instead, he sees a house at the back of the village behind the central square.

It is smaller than the rest, with a little picket fence that encloses the front door and a thatched roof that looks rotten. He limps over, creaking the fence on its broken hinge and stopping before the entrance, staring at the open latch. He holds out his hand, breathes in a sigh, and pushes through.

It creaks, and a shuffle can be heard from within. "Who is that?" A male voice groans from deeper within the house.

Saracen stands in the doorway and looks around the room, heartbroken. The sight of his once-beautiful childhood home is in tatters. Mold grows on the wooden walls, eating its way through, revealing the forest on the other side. A stray rug lies on the floor, positioned so that it is underneath a hole in the ceiling. It lies damp and adds to the smell of soiled grime. The smell saturates the air like salt in a granary, making it uneasy to breathe.

"Whoever it is, name yourself."

Saracen gives no response. He does not want to reply merely to find the source of the conversation. His feet follow his ears, sensing his way to the source through familiar structures, avoiding creaking floorboards and peeking around corners, searching for the owner of the voice.

"Please, just take what you want and leave."

There, lying on the floor, propped up against the wall within the bedroom, is a man with golden hair diluted by age. His hooded eyes, cradled with crow's feet, are a hazy white, looking out coldly to the dark.

"It's me, Father. It's Saracen."

The man's eyes follow the sound, as he looks at him in the doorway. "My boy?" Tears fall from his eyes as he holds out his wrinkled and bony hand, while his other continues to hold onto his chest. "Has my boy returned to me? Or is this a trick?"

Saracen looks upon his father, assessing his physical appearance and sees him staring out to the wind, frantically looking for an answer with his ears. He stands like a lost soul with dirty, worn clothes, with frayed patchwork on his breeches and dried, crusty skin.

"Yes, Father."

Saracen walks to him and crouches over, grasping hold of his father's hand with his own, carefully adjusting his balance with his stump. Since his pilgrimage to his father, his core muscles have grown in strength, adjusting to balancing with one arm; the extra challenge of holding his father's hand wouldn't have been possible a couple of weeks ago. The old man smiles, wearing it with pride and sniffling through his tears.

"My boy!"

After all these years, they embrace each other as best they can, becoming aware of each other's frailty, scars, and disabilities. Both cry in joy and the pain of lost time, immersed in emotion. The old man's hand goes back to his chest, revealing a day-old wound which has already begun to fester as flecks of green tarnish his skin and lick his clothing.

"Father, you're hurt. The wound is infected."

The man smiles at Saracen. "I know, my boy. I don't want to talk about that. I want to talk about your life. Tell me of your adventures. Are you happy? Are you safe?"

The man's hand rubs against Saracen's stump. Sorrowed and scared, his eyes carry a heavy weight under them.

"Saracen, my boy, what happened?

Saracen paused. "The war, Father. I was lucky to make it out alive. I remember the face of the man who did this to me."

His father strokes his son's face. "So, you are a knight. You made your childhood dreams a reality, and I am so proud of you." The old man shuffled in pain, propping himself up against the wall.

"Father, we have to get you to a herbalist, medicine man, or surgeon now."

Saracen begins lifting him with his arm underneath his shoulder, balancing himself against the wall with his stump as he does, but his father screams in agony, and the wound reopens, oozing out fluid.

"My boy, my life is complete. I have raised a beautiful man, who aspires for great things. Who is sharp of mind and strives to be something better. Who seeks to nurture greatness in other people. I want nothing more in my last breaths but to spend it with you, hear your songs and your tales so that I can go to the crossroads in the heavens and tell them to your mother on the long roads."

Saracen sits opposite him. "But we have to try? We have to try and make you well?"

The old man contemplates his words, pausing before responding with a smile. "I would likely be dead by the morning, and you know that."

Saracen looks to his father, a fragile old man with milky white eyes, stained ragged clothing, and an unkept beard. His hair strangled his back, unbrushed and filled with lice. But he smiled at him, a man he knew who did everything for him as a child. A man who raised him as a single father after his mother died in childbirth. He was, to Saracen, the greatest hero of them all. Beyond all the tales and songs of legend.

And so, he began to talk. He spoke about his life growing up as a squire, talking about the times he was scolded for sneaking out to see the girls in the courtyard. He spoke about the many hard times but most importantly, the many overwhelming good times. His father had many questions and was so curious to know more about the life of Saracen Murdock. The conversation was equally shared by both at first. The battles and the fun in recent times, vividly animated and told, so his father had to ask fewer questions, becoming weary as the night drew on.

It wasn't until the sun started to rise above the clearing, with the rays of light that began misbehaving their way through the holes in the ceiling that Saracen realized he never asked about his father. He never asked about the troubles he faced, what journeys he had had while he had been gone. But, alas, maybe some stories are not meant to be told.

Saracen's Father died there in front of his son, who he had not seen for

20 years. Through every song sung in childhood about heroes and their adventures or through their good deeds, Saracen always looked to the man reciting these tales as the real hero. He fended for them both when times were tough.

When food was scarce, he fished in the rivers just so Saracen could go to sleep at night with something in his stomach. When his clothes were left ripped from playing in the brook after being caught on the jagged rocks and twigs, he used his own clothes to repair and mend them.

The man was selfless, caring not for himself and only for his son's survival and flourishment. He wanted him to be the best he could be in the world so that one day, when Saracen was to bring children into the world, he would be able to give them the life he always dreamed that his son would have.

Saracen's mind began to fester with painful thoughts, ones that carried tears into his psyche, rendering his perception useless. Why did he not come back before? Why did his father not write to him to tell him he was struggling? He was torturing himself with what could have been, becoming angrier and angrier first with his father, then with himself as the darkest emotions of guilt and self-loathing took hold of him.

He was selfish, following his ambitions without a thought for his father who had given him all that he had - time, shelter, food and love. His quest to be better and nurture others to be the best they could be was a masquerade. He had thrived on destroying people, killing them by sword or command devoid of all feeling. His father had wanted grandchildren that had a better life than he had given him. He had failed to have even given him that. He had produced no heir and had no meaningful relationship with anyone. There were many women, yet mostly those who had fallen on hard times doing others' bidding, nonsignificant. The darkness crept through him, consumed him, eating away at his achievements, making them rotten.

Saracen Murdock the knight died that day, Saracen Murdock the man remained, hollowed, humbled and enraged.

16

Martha Honoroa - 32 Years Ago

The sky is an ashen gray, scarred by recent blue flickers from elf tear magic that has been set off to disburse the defenders from the walls. The fortifications lie in rubble, which smothers the homes and livelihoods of all those brave enough to stay in their houses, now lying in heaps so close to the front gate.

The flag of Honoroa flutters in the wind, burning with licks of white light, scattering ash into the wind as they are carried into the darkened distance. Arrows rain from the sky, landing into retreating soldiers and civilians attempting to seek shelter from the second line of defenses that hug the port and house the palace of Kings and Queens.

Civilians and soldiers alike begin to pour into the palace grounds, turning their heads as loved ones and friends are murdered like vermin, being cut down or impaled by raining arrows and bolts. The flag of the Crusaders covers the main road leading from the primary city gate, hoisting its colors like a righteous cause. But there is no righteousness in murdering innocent people.

Crusaders of the Pathlands burst through people's homes, prying any from their houses who are foolish enough to stay and murdering them in the street, or raping them in their beds if a pretty face or buxom beauty has hardened their loins. The spoils of war – if you happen to be the first to reach the dwelling, you have the first pick, or go – the fresh flesh. Sometimes you'd strike gold and be the first ever.

Honoroa does not have the resources to defend itself, does not have the men to hold them back, nor do they have any reinforcements coming. They are alone. The spice fields were a slaughter.

"Fall back to the palace! Fall back!"

Knights in bright white armor push back from the front lines, accompanying the injured through the palace doors and bolstering the garrison and militia with more weaponry and ammunition for their quivers from the palace arsenal.

There, amongst them, is Martha Honoroa, Princess and Captain of the Honor Guard of the Well Wood Tree and King's palace. They are the last hope for Honoroa, and usually, when they don the white armor of Honor, death swiftly follows. They are oath-sworn to protect the people and the city at all costs. Until their last breath.

"Your Royal Highness, the King has requested your audience in the Throne Room. They will be evacuating soon, and your children want to say goodbye." A tall woman in thick, chalk-like steel armor braces the door after bowing to the Princess, her helmet blackened by elf tear magic.

Martha looks deeply at the wooden frame, watching as men and women of the Honor Guard begin to bar it shut with whatever implements they can find. This is the only way through to the royal docks, and this is where they will hold them.

She stops and begins to trek into the palace, entering the courtyard. Dazzling gleams of sickly white light shine up from the Well Wood tree, penetrating the center of the courtyard, illuminating a magnificent display of dawn breaking into the palace.

Today, of all days, it shines brighter than the sun. Maybe it is commemorating the dead and shining brighter to guide them to the paths.

She pushes past, spotting more civilians saying goodbye to their dead relatives before leaving for the docks. Others are too paralyzed by their loss, grieving with red eyes and killing themselves with festering thoughts and denial.

The palace doors are open, and the King's Guard rallies in the halls with blue capes, white armor, tower shields, and silver spears that twist like willow bark.

She enters the hallway, moving herself through the guardsmen who salute her entry.

The palace is grand, with golden windows that tower its walls, letting in the light of day, a dark stone that is glossed with a hint of varnish, while beautiful sculptures and paintings decorate the walls.

The King sits on his throne, with his chest and stomach on show while medicine men stitch and dress his wound, which still bleeds even after three days from the Battle of the spice fields. His old, frail hand holds out for the Queen who sits next to him, worried, while she cradles a young baby girl in her arms.

"How is she?"

Martha stops before the seats, exposing herself to everyone in the room. Royalty and plebeian alike.

"She's fine. The wet nurse just left to pack for the voyage."

The Queen looks down from the speech to tickle the baby girl under the chin.

"And what of Jezel?"

A heavy sigh emits from the King's chest as he props himself to the back of the chair.

"He's with half of my personal guard and on a ship already, Martha. They left before the assault began."

The King splutters, coughing out chunks of blood from his tired body. The Queen grips tighter on the King's hand as she looks back to Martha with a worried face.

"Are you coming?"

The King weezes then turns to the Queen. "That is not happening."

The King continues to cough.

"But you make the rules of the kingdom? This is your world; this is your domain?"

Queen Lorraine watches her husband's face drop. He wheezes under his breath but gives an unsatisfactory shake of the head.

"Our ancestors made this Oath before the elves left Caldaria. If the Gods choose to save you, Martha…"

He turns his head.

"…Then they will choose to save you. It is not our decision to make."

A silence is drawn over the palace, with the distant sound of murder, destruction, and desolation in the distance. A pair of footsteps is heard making its way up the stairs.

"The ships are ready, Your Grace."

One of the King's Guard pants heavily after the long run.

"Then we leave with urgency for the free kingdom. Our allies there will hide our identity until it is time to strike and retake these lands, or at the very least, enact a thundering vengeance…"

He struggles to stand and moves his way down the stairs that slope towards the thrones, with stitching still being done on his ripped skin. He puts his hand down to his sheath and draws a white blade, glimmering with a sparkling light. "Protect this palace and do your Ancestors proud, dear Daughter."

Martha takes the blade, The Sword of Honor. The ancestral weapon of her people. She looks at the engravings made upon the steel, carved in ancient elven runes, and one of the few elven artifacts left in existence.

The Queen meets them down the steps and hands the baby girl to Martha, who cherishes the closeness, the sight, and the smell of her child. The baby girl looks up and smiles at the receipt of her mother's face.

"We thought we would name her after you. After her mother. Seeming as though you haven't decided on a name yet."

Martha smiles and kisses her deeply on the forehead, embracing her all before passing her back.

"I love you, sweet girl. I will meet you in the next life."

She turns and faces away, hiding her tears from her father and mother before moving towards the front gate with the others. She turns her head, watching them rush towards the docks and out of sight with the King's Guard following swiftly behind them.

"It's been a pleasure serving with you all. I would not wish for a better group of people to die with." The knights all line behind her and listen as the Crusaders begin to smash at the door with a makeshift ram.

"Your Majesty, we have a message from the Queen of Gesantia."

Martha turns her head, watching all the knights lower their visors.

The woman with the chalk armor stabs her in the back, crippling her to the ground.

The others head to the door and unbarricade it.

"I don't understand. What is the meaning of this?" Martha holds her back, as it bleeds a heavy pour of fresh blood.

"You really think we would die with you here? You fucking heretic." Martha goes to unsheathe her blade, but one of the knights holds out an elf tear and watches the light hit her like a wave, shattering her arm.

She screams in agony.

Crusaders begin to pour into the palace, armed with crossbows and covered in the colors of the Paths. A white painted armor with a black wayward marker on the crossroads on a pale grey tabard.

"Well, well, well, if it isn't the Princess of Honoroa, how delighted I am to meet you."

A tall blond woman with regal attire and fashionable armor struts in with a blood-covered blade. She looks to the knights in white.

"You've satisfied one end of the bargain, now where is the other half?" The tall blond woman wipes her blade clean on her clothes.

"No, Your Grace, they escaped. They had the entire King's Guard with them."

The blond-haired woman tuts and wags her finger. She looks over to her crossbowman and nods her head, watching them point, aim, and pepper the knights with bolts that pierce through their armor like a hot knife through butter.

"No matter, I have what I want." She looks down to Martha and bends her knees.

"You're going to do perfectly fine for my child when he gets out..." She taps her stomach.

"And then, after the marriage and binding magic, we will torture you until you tell us where your family went, and if you don't talk…"

Her face goes from talking softly to now being firmer. "…We will make you talk."

17

Lady Alayna Astravix - Give Quietly, Love Deeply

Alayna stands up from the chair in shock as the guardsmen surround Jezel, pinning him to his knees and looking up to Arrabella. The crowd gasps, with whispers of the word heresy chittering from their lips.

"So, your family is still with us? Well not for long" She quietly and calmly whispers in Martha's ear, just loud enough for Alayna to hear. "No matter, I will see to it that we finish the job this time and that we wipe your blood line off Caldaria once and for all. I am so glad he came to see you. I am so glad you are alive to witness this."

Arrabella looks at Martha who stands from her chair glaring back at her with disgust.

"Jezel, why did you come here?" Martha turns her head in worry.

"Why did you risk your life like this?"

Arrabella casts her arm out and slaps Martha across the face, sending her to the floor and then Arrabella looks to the crowd.

"Guards! I want him in the dungeon NOW! We cannot have a heretic at my daughter's choosing ceremony!"

She then looks to Martha. "I will personally cut his head clean of his body, so I know your bloodline is gone. And you will watch and then clean up the blood afterwards after you carry his corpse to the dogs."

Jezel looks to the pulpit, and sniggers before he addresses the crowd.

"Why is it that you need to put me in your dungeon, which I am sure don't intend for me to leave alive? What reason am I a threat to the Pathlands now that my kingdom is destroyed, my culture, our values?"

Hands grab at his shoulders as guardsmen begin to drag him by the arms through the dirt.

"What have I done to you? I was a child when the war began and ever since then you have tried to hunt down me and my family, wiping them out from existence?"

The crowd's whispers stop, elevating a silent ring as Arrabella looks to the guards gripping him tightly by the arm.

"Wait."

Anger swells in her eyes, filling her mind with thought.

"Mumma." Jezel looks to Martha. "We live." He pauses. "We are safe."

Martha stares out to her son and lets out a wail before falling to her knees. "Why? Why are you telling them? They will only try and hunt us down again? I have gone through so much to hide this secret."

Jezel smiles to Arrabella, smirking a grin, one of justice or more sinisterly, vengeance.

"Kill him!" Arrabella arches her hand and points to Jezel. "Kill him now!

The guardsman raises his sword into the air as the other two push his neck to the floor. But, sometimes, fate has another plan in store for us.

From the kitchens in the castle, an explosion of blue energy erupts from within. The fire reaches the clouds, sending rock and debris into the air which comes quickly crashing back down around the tourney grounds. And with the fire, a haze of what looks like glittering stars, rains down like heated ash.

Martha is shaken but her mind turns to the hole in the wall and her thoughts race. Was this part of a plan to free her after all these years? Or was it something sinister.

Alayna's ears ring from the madness, as she watches rocks crash down into the crowd, some no bigger than a gold piece, others as big as a horse.

The crowds begin to disperse, running frantically for overhead protection as members of the audience are crushed under falling stone.

In the chaos, Alayna looks over to where Jezel was captured to see his captors lying lifeless on the floor as blood spills against the ground. The knight was nowhere to be seen. A guardsman rushed towards Alayna, grabbing her arm and raising a shield over her head to cover their retreat. "Come with me my Lady." He spirits her away as fast as he can, doing his job by separating her from Martha and her mother.

Darting down the stairs as the debris falls around them, they just make it before a crowd of people come hurtling out of the shade of the pavilion tent. Panic had set in; people were in full flight trying to avoid their bodies being added to the corpses that litter the grounds.

Alayna's feet come loose from her shoes as she struggles through the crowd with the guardsman. She was dressed in finery not swift movement, and it hindered her. Her feet now feel the blades of grass against her toes, and she lifts her dress up higher from the floor being careful not to trip.

Another explosion is heard, this time from deeper within the castle grounds, lifting yet again more debris into the sky and raining a sickly haze over the castle grounds. Alayna runs with the crowd, the sound of rushing feet and cries become piercing. Her guard firmly grips her arm as they push towards more overhead cover.

It's a horrific scene, where men and women are screaming, already mourning the dead that litter the ground. Some children cry alone over fallen parents while the injured crawl away gripping at passers-by for help. One minute, partying and enjoying the pleasantries. Next, dead.

A smell begins to fill the air as a sickly perfume burns the noses of everyone unlucky enough to breath it's in. An unnatural smell. A synthetic smell. Alayna covers her mouth and nose with her hand as the crowd begins to rush further through the castle grounds towards the main gatehouse.

Around the corner, thirty or so men in crimson robes bearing the mark of the broken tower hold blades in their hands, advancing at pace towards the scared crowd. Both parties stop and stare before the cultists charge towards them. The crowd screams again as it turns and makes its way back towards the tourney grounds with the men at their tail.

People begin to fall, as they are carved through like meat at a butcher. No remorse for gender, status or age. All are slain, all fall and are stamped on beneath the feet of many.

The guardsman guides her on towards cover with some others, not back to the grounds, swerving to the right, away from the charging rebels. Alayna's hand comes loose from the guardsman in the crowd as he falls to the floor. She continues running forward with the crowd looking over her shoulder trying to spot the guard. She caught a glimpse of him swinging his sword frantically and covering his face with his shield before the cultists make quick work and slaughter him like a pig, cutting his throat and ramming a blade inside his chest.

The crowd continues at pace as Alayna is pulled along in the chaos. They make their way through the castle courtyard and into the feasting hall which burns a blue flame. Some barricade the doors while others disperse further into the castle's guts.

Alayna runs for her bedroom. Stamping up the stone steps barefoot and along the creaking solid wooden floorboards, she makes her way along the hallway and into her room, slamming the door shut behind her.

"Hello flower." Alayna turns her head to a familiar voice, seeing Martha sitting on the bed, grasping at her bloodied arm.

"Mumma, are you okay? How did you get up here?"

Martha nods. "Oh, I know every nook and cranny of this castle. Your mother had me clean it all before with a broken brush as punishment many a time. I can get around fairly easily."

"Are you hurt?"

She smiles as a response, ignoring the question. "That was my son, Jezel."

She turns her head away. "I haven't seen him since he was a baby, but I recognise the scar on his face."

Alayna sits next to her and holds her hand while Martha smiles. "It's good he's alive Martha."

Martha looks back to Alayna and gasps as another explosion is heard from somewhere in the castle erupting and echoing through halls and shaking the limestone bricks all while dust falls from the heights of the ceiling.

"Pack your things. We need to try and get out of here flower."

Alayna rushes up, grasping hold of a leather backpack and ramming clothes into it. She places it onto the bed and makes sure to pack the items for Martha. But the door opens, and a shadow lurks in its place.

"Martha Honoroa?"

It was deep, gloomy and filled with hate.

"Yes, who is talking?"

Two more shadows come through the door, holding daggers in their hands.

"The future is talking."

Martha looks to Alayna and shows a side to her that Alayna has never seen.

The men burst in, grabbing Martha by the hand and pulling her back towards them so that her head looks towards Alayna. She shows little resistance, may it be her age, her strength or her will. His hand reaches for his belt as he draws a dagger carved in runes and jagged slots reaching for her stomach, pointing at her kidney and then her stomach as the blade trickles against her dress. Martha looks down, then trails the steel up the shaft and past the intruders arm to see Alaynas face.

"I love you Flower."

She smiles, watching the arm cascade into her stomach.

A gush, an exhale then a gasp for air as Martha lets out a little groan. There was no elegance about it, only a thrashing of anger and hatred as the dagger was taken out and then rammed into another section of her body.

Blood begins to spill from Martha's mouth as her glare meets Alayna's eyes, while the dagger plunges into her chest and then stomach for the sixth time.

Alayna petrified, now begins to push forward, charging towards the door attempting to force her way past the other two men. Side stepping to the left, jumping in her tight choosing dress over the bedside table, knocking it to the floor due to her stiff corset. One of the men grab her arm, lifting her up, guarding their face as Alayna releases a slap before he then throws her onto the bed.

"What do we have here?" The murderer said.

He wipes his dagger on his robe, letting Martha fall from his grip to the floor, cleaning her blood from the blade before wiping the moisture from his mouth with his sleeve as he begins to unbutton his trousers. The two men grab her arms and pin her down to the bed breathing heavily under their lips, she could smell their breath and feel their strength. Alayna screams flailing her legs but cannot move. She does everything in her power to make this hard by arching her back.

"Your feisty. I like feisty."

A bloodstained finger, rolls against the exposed flesh on her leg, pushing his weight against her thighs and dress. Another, grabs her dress, tearing it to see more.

"I aint tried a noble yet. Bet you taste like elderberries." he smiles, now gripping her leg with a a full force, as his nails dig in to her flesh. Alayna sinks into the bed, still pushing back with as much force as she can give. But nothing works. It was hopeless. She bellows, but one of the other men presses his hand over her mouth.

The murderer looks forwards now, towards her eyes. Staring blankly into her soul, vying to get a piece of it. He smiles.

"What a pretty face. Such a shame."

His finger runs up towards her briefs and then he grips tightly, running them down her leg as he manoveurs his body up towards her chest.

The attack is swift, accurate and just in time.

A blade, forces its way through the mans face cleanly between the eyes. It then retracts, splurting blood as it relieves itself as the body falls limp onto Alayna.

Alayna is too shocked to scream, she breaths in heavy fast breaths, as the blood and brains splatter across her face which runs down across her eyes and over her mouth. Even after those that held her down release her to fend for their lives, she is frozen to the bed unable to move or speak, struggling to breath.

She stared blankly towards the door, these men remained a mystery as her eyes only saw a blurry visage, a haze, all while her ears sang a high-pitched ringing sound. She turned her head, focusing on the ground where a puddle of blood filled the room. She trailed it to a woman lying on the floor, eyes open and no longer choking on her own blood. The woman who had nursed her, attended to her and showed her the only motherly kindness she'd known was dead.

Martha Honoroa, the rightful ruler of the Kingdom of Honoria, was gone.

And a dark time for Gesantia, and the rest of Caldaria, was to follow.

18

Arelle Goodsberry - The Baby and the Baron

Osric and Arelle made their way out of the tavern after grabbing what food they could find, turning their heads to watch their corners as they swiftly moved out of the village into the foliage.

They slipped away unseen, as the Barons' henchmen flooded the streets, beating on doors and forcing their way into homes. They both move quietly and quickly, continuing their journey into the wilderness.

The trees swayed in the wind, whistling to each other, speaking of songs and stories that happen in these woods. I suppose, they speak of the same old stories, but before the week is done, they will be gossiping amongst each other like old ladies.

Some time then passes.

A light flicker from deep inside the cave as both Arelle and Osric manoeuvre through the thick blanket of snow that covers the land.

"Is that it?" Arelle grabs hold of Osric's arm, steadying herself as she carefully chooses her steps.

"Yes, that's the one. Stay close. The orc will be vigilant of strangers and the last thing we want is you dead."

Arelle doesn't reply. She just holds Osric's arm tightly, keeping her eyes on her footwork and towards the path ahead. Moment's pass, and the two descend into the cave's mouth as it reveals Urg-Tor holding a young baby orc boy in his arms.

"Who's that?" Urg calms the baby boy, cradling him over his shoulder while his eyes fix onto Arelle. She eats her words at first but takes a moment before letting them out.

"I am here to help."

The orc looks with his brow lowered, piercing through Arelle's essence, judging every movement, even her muscular twitches in her face. Osric steps forward, looking over his shoulder to Arelle and then back to Urg.

"I have made some headway onto what is going on, and if the matter wasn't pressing, I would discuss these things with you. But we don't have time."

Osric tosses him a leather satchel filled with a cornucopia of food.

The orc stands strong catching the bag filled with food in his hands, towering over the group but the fear from his eyes tears his demeanour in two. He reaches into the satchel, grasping hold of some dried meat and begins to feed the baby in his arms.

"What of it human? Did you find my wife? Did you find Tenya?"

Arelle looks to Osric, standing with his back straight.

"Urg, I couldn't see her."

The orcs scrunches his face and looks down on the human, awaiting a better response.

"The Baron had sent someone to watch me come out of the cave and kill me if I didn't have your head. He also delivered a poisonous speech and the townsfolk have risen up to march towards this place by the morning. We must leave now Urg. There is nothing we can do for your wife at the moment."

The orc puts down the now settled baby, swaddling him in scraps of leather and wool. He paces towards Osric then stands over him looking down.

"Maybe I was wrong about you. Maybe, you're just like the rest of them. Like the rest of your kind."

Osric looks up to meet Urg's eyes but before words could come out of his mouth, the orc snaps. "She is my wife, Osric. My wife."

His finger slams against his own chest.

"In my culture, we would die for them. Sacrificing everything. We scream life in the face and charge towards the threat. It is in our blood, human."

Osric closes his eyes, sighs and reopens them. "And what of your son? What would you do if he was left fatherless and motherless? What then?"

Urg arches his back, clenching his fist all while pushing his veins beyond their limits, pressing against his pale burgundy skin. The baby coos and the orc turns, lowering his head looking down towards the child.

"Is that the future you want for him?"

Arelle watches as Osric stands next to him, peering down at the young boy.

"I want a future for my whole family, Osric. I want us to thrive in this life. But so many things and people are hurdles along the way."

Urg bends down, releasing the baby from his makeshift cradle and looks to both Arelle and Osric and with which he enters his pocket with his hand. He pulls out Osric's Elf tear and smiles at them both with a grin of hope and fear.

"Humans, what do I have to do to save my family?"

Sir Osric takes the elf tear from him, and peers at the baby.

"Earlier today, I sent a Raven to my order and to the high council in Xanathose requesting immediate aid. If we head to Octon vale, a village just two days' travel south, we can meet them there and then I will personally help retrieve Tenya but for now we must retreat. There is a fishing harbour a few hours to the east, we can use one of the boats to escape."

Arelle, far too busy listening to the coos of the baby, looks to both Osric and Urg discussing each other's plans going forward. The baby looks in her direction and his face becomes dead serious.

Urg looks down and then up following the baby's vision. He smiles. "In my culture young human, that means the baby sees you as someone with a strong heart. Wear that thought with pride."

Urg looks back to Osric. "It is decided then. We will head South, but first we must get as many supplies as we can muster from here..."

Osric nods confirmingly. "Agreed."

Leather bags are wrapped with sleeping rags, dried foods and meat, a hand axe and other travelling gear before all three begin congregating back in the caves entrance just outside the orcs' makeshift house.

Urg wraps the baby in a swaddle before handing him to Arelle.

"If we are attacked human, I want to rip the hearts out from those that took my wife. I cannot do that with a child on my other arm although I most definitely would try."

The baby coo's wriggling his arms and legs around adjusting to the new posture while Arelle manoeuvres him carefully in her arms.

"I will make sure to keep him safe."

Arelle says, while anxiously looking back at him, arching her neck up to meet his gaze.

Osric puts a backpack on and looks to the other two. "Are we ready?"

They both nod in agreement and follow the pathway out towards the cave's mouth and into the breath of the lurking cold that awaits them.

Urg looks at Arelle one last time while within the flicker of a torch light. She is chattering away with his baby, making him comfortable as she adjusts to the extra load. The consistent concerned expression on Urg's face, relieves a smile just for a moment. Although anxious for the future, he is comforted by the humans' tenderness to his son.

The party begins the long trudging through the snow, wading their way through untamed wilds and as the hours begin to pass and the sun begins to sleep, the smell of salt water begins to fill their nostrils as they see little fishing boats bob in the cold icy water that swells against the rocky edge.

As they approach the clearing, Osric hears something in the distance and fears the worst. He draws his sword and steps in front of Arelle, cautious now. He indicates quiet to the party, lowering his hand for them all to take a knee. The orc draws his axe ready for action and joins Osric in the front both now shielding Arelle and the baby.

They have reached the harbour but as they do, the source of the noise is revealed, and Osric's fears are confirmed. There are many torches flickering in the night, coming their way hungry to light the path towards them. Snapping up the air from around them reveals the shadows of humans carrying pitchforks and makeshift weapons. They were closing in on them fast.

"Get in the boat Arelle, and if diplomacy fails, get the fuck out of here."

Arelle looks down to the baby and then to Urg who walks over to them both. Urg rubs the babies head.

"If we fail today, go to my people in the Zafrazzi plains. Tell them you have Jay Tor, son of Urg tor and Tenya. They will honour him as one of their own and you will be rewarded."

Urg bends down to kiss baby Jay on the cheek. "I love you my son, I hope this is not the day we part."

Arelle doesn't respond, but looks to the two large figures, one man, one orc readying their weapons and standing in the cold dark while the snow begins to fall atop their heads.

"If we go now, we can all make it before they get here."

Arelle clings to some hope. A hope that wants to latch onto.

"They would catch up to us, Arelle."

Osric looks to her.

"Go, we will buy you the time you need."

In the distance, the lies that were spread, have multiplied like bacteria and filled the town with darkness, they were sharpening their teeth and ready to do things they never would have before. Their hateful cries begin to be heard searing the minds and hearts of those that heard them. Arelle had doubts before, doubts about her father caused by the flicker of hope that burnt within her. But that flicker was dead, she doubted no longer.

The people of the village begin their approach, casting long shadows between the trees as the sun falls to the ground, leaving the chattering of maniacal choruses to play.

"I think I see something at the harbour"

"Yes, definitely not human"

They quicken their pace, excited that they think the prey of their hunt is found.

The trees will have their gossip after all.

19

Koga - Beyond the Sea

The plains rolled with seas of yellow grass, waving in the not so gentle breeze. It carried a foul taste in it, not one of death, not yet, but one of turning flesh. The two brothers were used to it, it had become as normal as the air they breathed and had been like this for at least 12 moons.

Recently though, it has started getting worse, sticking to the chest like a fever.

The world is sick. Each breath was hard to take in. The air, like humidified acid, leeching the energy from every step, pushing against your chest enveloping you and everyone you love.

Ever since the elves left, nothing has been the same.

But, before even that time, before the time the elves left this world and more towards the time that they surrounded the lands of Caldaria with their great empire, The Zafrazzi lived together in harmony and union in the untamed lands to the south. Orc and Landari aligned themselves with each other, creating a cultural marvel that shone like a beacon creating jealous rival tribes.

From what history they do have, the Zafrazzi came about through defence against the ever-expanding elven empire that sought control and dominion of the rolling fields of the Zafrazzi plains. But, even with magic, the elves met their match. For you cannot beat the Zafrazzi. They will never seek defeat as an option and to them, death was the start of a longer journey.

The sun beams fought their way through the thick haze of clouds on the horizon as the frail wind moaned on the Zafrazzi plains this morning, whistling through the tall thick yellow grass of the Savannah.

Sitting on the ground was a tall nine-foot lion man, staring at the haze as he sharpened his spear with a lump of thick flint. He had a large mane with flicks of red trickles that enchant his face and give homage to his eyes. His hands were larger than a human baby, while his claws were as big as human fingers.

His people are called the Landari, an ancient species of lion who woke from their primitive lives many, many moons ago. Some say it was magic that made them evolve their species. Others say it was Caldaria's blessing.

"Leandro, brother." A large dark Burgundian orc wearing woven clothes of reeds and carrying a stone axe walks over. He smiled at Leandro, pleased to see him and wondered what he was worried about. He could always tell by the look on his face.

"Koga. "Leandro smiles back.

"Any news on the hunt? When did the chief say we can start."?

Koga sits next to him, letting his arm rest on his bent knee, staring out to the horizon while his other hand plays with the grass picking up pieces of yellow strands and watching them turn to dust as he rubs them between his fingers.

"Soon."

He turns to Leandro. "I'm going to bag myself a big kill this year, better than last. Maybe the chief will let me sit with him at the feast while you sit amongst the shit."

Koga slaps Leandro on the shoulder, chuckling a heavy laugh. "After eating as much as you did last year, I'm sure it will be you, you pig."

They both share a chuckle back.

"So, where shall we go this year, Leandro? East? Big buffalo that way. Or are we heading West like last year? Giant armadillos roam those parts, just like the one you snapped up."

Leandro stands, noticing the mists begin to get thicker across the horizon. "Nothing has been roaming these lands for four moons now, Koga. I'm worried we won't get anything."

Koga stands with him, curious to what he's looking at but continuing the conversation regardless. "I heard Daka said he saw white bucks two weeks ago at the forked cliffs. But you're right, I haven't seen animals for some time. Why do you think that is? and where do you think they have gone, Leandro?"

"I'm not sure Koga. But I think we should head south."

Koga walks into his field of vision, staring at him like he's a mad man. "Have you lost your mind? Do you want to lose your head? Or worse. Become Zaffaza?"

"Zaffaza? You really think they will make us Prideless for being so curious? You really think the people of our tribe will cast us out like that?"

Leandro tuts his lips and then places his hand onto Koga's shoulders. "I want to find out why the clouds are falling, Koga. Why the plains are not like they once were. And besides, there might be creatures that dwarf the ones the others bring. Or maybe, great treasures await us. No one goes down there so no one would know? "

Koga stares at Leandro from eye to eye waiting for him to laugh, but then realisation hits. He was being serious. "That is because it is forbidden to go there. We may enter the land of Minos and start the war again which the chief worked so hard in trying to make peace with?"

The orc grunts, and turns his head towards the plains. 'That chief of ours sure does love peace. Why does he go against everything we stand for? These are our plains. Our land. Our home. Not Minos'. He is not fit to rule."

Leandro looks to his blood brother. "Is that the life you want, Koga? A life where we live as serfs to a Lord? Like a human? We may as well be Zaffaza. We may as well have no pride at all."

Koga sighs and lowers his head. "Your right. I'm sorry to question you. You know my mind steers."

Leandro puts his hand atop Koga's shoulder. "Don't be sorry. Sometimes I need you to keep me in check too. Always question me, I need that from someone I trust."

A horn sounds from the distance, calling for the start of the great hunt.

On the horizon, great warriors atop of giant large spotted dog like creatures, with snarling snouts and fluffy haired backs charge into different directions, screaming Zu Zhata Zafrazzi which loosely translates to 'What a beautiful day to die for Pride'. Eager for fresh blood, for the kill of the year so that one day their coats will line the hall of great ones.

"Come brother, for we must be quick if we want people to sing songs of us around the campfire." Leandro lifts his head as he looks towards the haze to the south and watches as Koga gets the first couple of steps in front of him, ushering him to follow, pointing south while the hordes head in other directions.

Both were excited, with springs in their step and hands clenched on their weapons. As they charge in the direction, they both scream at the top of their voice Zu Zhata Zafrazzi, to echo their brothers in the field. The Zafrazzi Prides began pouring out of the leather tents and huts, armed with stone axes and wooden spears.

Leandro and Koga stop their movement within a tall bundle of savannah grass and lay within it to watch the last tribesmen leave and head into the distance.

"Let us give it a while before we head further south, we don't want to draw attention to ourselves."

Koga nods in a happy fury, but deep down, Leandro had a fear that something more was to be told about this haze that smothered the sky.

Something dire.

20

Saracen Murdock - The Walk to the Well Wood

A termite scurries across the rotted floor, scratching at the wood as it etches through the soft coating and into its hive below with its fellow brethren. The smell of rotten, mossy wood awakens the senses as the sun shines across the little run-down home.

Saracen weeps atop his father, the passage of time becoming insignificant to his mind. His head rests on his chest, and incomprehensible words gush out from his mouth, with the hope someone is listening to him. The wound that took his father is already a festering mess, consuming the rest of him as the grimness of death fills Saracen's nostrils. The smell, like rotten chicken left out in the sun, and webby saliva, like strands, drip from his flesh.

All Saracen can feel is anger. It swells up within him as it clouds his mind and judgment. An anger that he blames on himself and his choices that led him to his fate today. His guilt, a vile parasite, eats away at him just like his father's wound. A plethora of questions haunt him, devouring his mind and torturing his soul.

He looks around him, taking in the surroundings and how his father lived. A shack of moss-covered walls and unkept furniture, with no regard for his own health. He should have been here; he should have been here to look after his father and to protect the village against the attack.

Right now, his spiral of emotions has succumbed to a sudden destiny of trouble as his failures begin to toy with him. He has failed.

He stands, and blood rushes to his head, filling his mind with a mist, poisoning his balance and posture. The thoughts continue though, playing on his wits. Through hazy, puffy eyes, he looks up through the cracks in the ceiling, watching birds on the trees sing, sitting on branches, telling morning tunes however their happy songs do not interest him.

His mind wanders deeper, and as it does, he moves with it, overwhelmed with guilt, a stain on his soul, a blade in his heart that will be there forever. He continues outside, trailing his dirty, worn feet across the floor, scraping them against the path as his tired legs struggle.

Why couldn't he have died there on the battlefield? He thinks. Why couldn't he have joined his father now, welcoming him on the paths with his mother? Caldaria is bent on making itself a dire place indeed, and it has no remorse for its actions.

He stumbles, falling over scattered corpses that line the street. Dead women and children who all seem to look at him in unison. Eyes like daggers that sweep the streets with their gaze. Reminders of his failure, reminders that he could have saved them all if he was here.

This ignites his anger further; he pushes himself back to his feet and stares back at them.

"Why did you run?" he says. "Why didn't you hide?"

The dead give no answer but look at him with rotted flesh and petrified faces.

His blood boils, struggling to get a grip of reality as he presses on through the village, while the corpses follow him with their eyes.

"Is this how reality will be? Dead lining the street, mothers dying with children hugging them for comfort while men die in war. Fighting for vengeance after being betrayed?"

He looks to the sky, eyes fixed on the clouds, praying out loud delivering his disgust to the gods.

"Where were you?" he pauses, "Why did you have to leave us?"

Tears of anger stream down his face. "Why? Why make orphans of children? What purpose do you give them if they die of hunger only days later?"

He slightly bends his neck and holds his hand over his forehead in despair.

"Why!"

He shouts, releasing a pulse of energy that vibrates across the floor. The earth seems to move like a wave as this huge rush of energy pours over the nearby buildings around him, bursting them into splinters and covering everything with a lick of blue fire. When the pulse dissipates into the surroundings, birds fly from the trees, chirping songs of fear and telling their friends and family to seek shelter.

He stumbles, unbalanced, and falls to his knees, unable to catch himself with his hand. His arm outstretched, while his eyes fix on his fingers that now dig into the rain and blood-moistened ground. His nails begin to hum with an unnatural guise of blue that begins to taint his very fingertips in a sickly tinge as a smell of a synthetic hue hums from them, burning his lungs if he brought his nose too close.

He can feel every spark leave his body, every vibration, every satisfactory ripple, as it dissipates as fast as it appeared.

That rush of energy. The release of power.

It feels wonderful. It feels fantastic...

Is this magic? A dream or a hallucination from his twisted mind? Whatever it is, he likes it and wishes by the gods he wasn't dreaming.

His mind runs through more questions, taking him away from his dark thoughts to those of curiosity. Was this the rush, the feeling, the euphoria that the elves had all those years ago? Like an addict heating the spoon and embracing its chase, toying with his sense and burning the very fire and core of his being with ecstatic pleasure and delights.

'No, it cannot be. I must have touched a discarded elf tear nearby,' he thinks.

He looks to his hand, staring as the bluish tint that begins to taint further down his fingertips glow, staining his skin with a colorless silk. But that wouldn't describe this?

Looking up from his gaze, the landscape begins to settle in the wind. A landscape that he once called his home is now razed in ruin, glowing in bluish flames that envelop the houses and wildlife around him. A perfect circle where the energy pulsed from within him shattered reality around, leaving it in a desolate state of destruction. The blacksmith at the end of town feels the fury, as the magical remnants of the forge light up again, churning out black smoke from the chimney spout.

He trudges back to his father, looking at the corpses that now lie with their eyes closed. Resting amongst the foliage and hugging their loved ones, with smiles on their faces.

'Did I do that too?'

Their bodies were not harmed, nor a flame that flickered around them. He stepped between the bodies, mesmerized by his hand but with eyes flickering to the road ahead.

Saracen stepped through his father's door, pushing it as it creaked against the warped wooden floor. He made his way to the back room and saw his father lying lifeless to the ground. Hope came to him in this dark place, however, and with it, he held his hand out over his father and closed his eyes. He had nothing to lose at this point and everything to gain.

At first, he felt nothing. Not even a tingle or vibration, let alone the intense power he felt before.

But with time, his fingers began to catch something, spinning, wrapping itself around them.

He was mesmerized, gripped by a force he could not understand. A force he could not explain. But one he knew was there.

He opened his eyes and saw his father standing in front of a Well Wood tree looking towards him. His wound was still festering. His eyes are still hazy. But he smiled. The Well Wood tree branches grew out in many directions. Some sparkled and spanned for miles, a huge network spiraling into many directions. But one seems to grow into Saracen's father's mind and beyond that the rest of the local branches made their way into the minds of others who walked around the area. He could see the roots it made against the side of his father's head, like deep veins or arteries.

"Father. Come with me." A smile. A man full of goodness, love, and pride.

His father walked towards him and held his hand out to touch his.

"You do not walk these paths alone my son".

Saracen blinked, and the image was gone, but he felt the presence there, as if he was embracing a handshake. He looked down to his father's body, who remained lifeless, still, and cold. The presence leaves, removing its clasp on Saracen, as if blowing into the wind, but yet Saracen feels more at peace.

He stands, continuing his gaze, but then turns back to the front door before stopping in the doorway and releasing a sigh of relief and sadness. His hand touches the arch, and using all of his thoughts, he ignites the warped wood in a blue flame. There was no point in burying him. He knew he was in a better place, and this is where he would have wanted to be anyway.

The evidence of the mysterious deed will be buried in ash and soot by the evening. A mystery that filled Saracen's thoughts, taking them away from his guilt and anger, something that may have answers out there in the wide world of Caldaria. "Why is it that he had the means to use magic and all those before him that are human could not?" He added this to the growing questions in his mind.

A single soul walked into the village late yesterday, and a single soul walked out. But it's possible that many souls still lurk there, waiting to be put to rest, and yet they do not know the way out.

21

Lady Alayna Astravix - Play with Fire

Martha lies on the floor with blood filling in her mouth, pouring onto the ground as it becomes too overwhelming to hold.

Three men with cloaks stare towards Alayna drooling, like grotesque shadows which almost cling to the creeping darkness in the corner of her vision. The shadows loom, plaguing her. She tries to claw at the bed, to move backwards, retreating into the pillows behind her but gains no ground. The shadows creep forward devouring the light they touch and dripping dark saliva onto her chest, leaving a black oil like residue that burns to the touch.

Claw-like fingers grip at her ankles, tightening their vice as they grow longer and fiercer, wrapping themselves around like tentacles. A flash or shimmer reflects the remaining light of the room, as a dagger is pulled from one of their visages and it pushes the blade through her throat, lapping up the blood that pours out of her neck like a blood feasting insect. She began to feel hazy, as a weight pushes against her body, eating away at her as her body gave in to its fate.

Alayna awakens screaming, sweaty and confused. She lay amongst a haystack pulled by a horse and cart along a cobbled road. The air was cool, as the breeze from the mountains rolled down the valley and through the forests. The road was bumpy, and the straw was scratchy, but somehow as she began to breathe the fresh country air, the confusion and sweat stopped as

Alayna's stomach began to float in the clouds, as her eyes watched Prince Joseph atop a brown mare. He wore a black chest plate with a muscular pattern on the stomach and the pictures of a golden tapestry displayed on his chest. He bites into a red apple, finishing the outer skin before tossing it into the brush and swallows his mouthful before looking at the rest of the men.

"Halt! Joseph snags at his reigns. "Lady Alayna is awake."

The wagon comes to a complete stop and the horses whine in anticipation. He dismounts and holds his hand out to Alayna.

"Sorry about the cart butterfly, unfortunately it was the only thing left in the chaos. Come, you can have my horse."

"What happened?"

Joseph rests his arms against the wagon, crossing them while continuing eye contact. "Rebels attacked the castle, burst through your door. We came in and saved you."

Alayna remembers the blood splattering against her face as the memory of that day begins to flood in like a nightmare. "Why would they do that? all those people... so many killed and Martha ...they asked who she was first, why?"

"They want a world about them. About their views and aspirations. So they try to destroy the world around them, the world our ancestors built."

Alayna begins to shake, almost like there is a chill. "Thank you for saving me."

Joseph smiles, standing on top of his stirrups and then proceeds to climb atop the wagon, putting an arm around Alaynas shoulders to provide warmth, wrapping his cloak around her for extra protection. "That's alright butterfly, we are here now and once we get to Astronozia the great city in Arudania, you will never have to worry again. We will keep you safe."

It was a strange mix of emotions that now filled Alayna's head, but the one that overwhelmed her the most, was the one she felt for Martha. She laid her head onto Joseph's chest, hiding her face from the soldiers who stood to attention.

"When you are ready to talk to me more, you just let me know, okay? I will always have time for you"

Alayna smiles, looking down to the hay that lies underneath her legs, spotting her torn dress she blushes, aware he can see more than is appropriate. That's when she notices the bruises on her legs both sides of each leg from her ankles up to her knees at various points. The ones made by being dragged back down the bed. The ones that paint the feelings and anxious thoughts she so hallowingly dreams about. She panics, breathing heavy breaths, right now, she needs Martha, her soft soothing velvety voice, hugs and herbal tea. The vision of her being stabbed so many times filled her thoughts.

"Why did they kill her?"

Alayna tries to rush to her feet, but Joseph stops her. She instantly begins bursting into tears, clawing at Joseph to embrace a hug.

"Woah, woah, easy." He brushes through her hair with his fingers.

"The men killed my maid, Martha. They asked who she was first - then killed her." She looked inquiringly at Joseph through floods of tears" Why would they do that?" She wasn't really thinking about what she said or seeking a response, just a sounding board as if saying it out loud helped it sink in.

Alayna struggles to lever herself from Joseph's shoulder but he grips her with all his might.

"Easy, easy."

Alayna no longer struggles but begins to hold Joseph and embrace him.

"Dimitri, tell the men we will camp here tonight."

A flick of some reigns and the snorting of a nearby horse flicks against their ears.

"Yes, your highness."

Orders are barked in the distance as the galloping of a horse is heard nearby.

"What happened to my mother? And the rest of my household? Alayna lifts her tear jerked head away from Joseph's shoulder and wipes at the red ducts with her sleeve. Joseph looks down to meet her eyes.

"Rebels Alayna. Rebels got them."

She looks back down to her bruised legs.

"We don't know much or how many died or were wounded. It will be a while before we know if there were survivors. Once we arrive at Astronozia I will send my best men to investigate and find out what has happened, and track down any of your family members. I assure you." He holds her shoulder.

"Let me get you some water and some food you must be starving." Jumping off the wagon he is stopped by a hand yanking him back.

"Don't leave me. They might come back and get me Joseph. They might try and do terrible things to me."

A concerned look meets her eyes. "Okay butterfly. I will get one of the men to come and serve us here and we can just sit and chat."

"Dimitri!"

An older looking soldier makes his way over from ordering the men, making haste as he follows the tone of his commander.

"Yes, your Highness."

"Bring me a loaf of bread and some dried tomatoes. Then have the men cook up a stew when they are ready."

Dimitri bows his head gently, then turns to Alayna.

"My Lady."

He turns and heads to a nearby horse and pulls out the goods required from a satchel before returning.

"Was there anything else your Highness? May I interest you in some wine?"

Joseph looks to Alayna who shakes her head.

"No, that will do fine Dimitri, as you were."

Joseph breaks off a portion of fresh bread and hands Alayna the container of dried tomatoes before they both indulge.

She sinks into both, not realising how hungry she was as she eats up as much as Joseph.

After they finish, Alayna then lowers her head onto his lap and stares out across the horizon.

"No one will hurt you. I will protect you. Do you understand?"

Alayna responds only with a tight grip onto his arm.

"I'm taking you to my home. Away from the war. Away from the fire and the fighting.

You will be safe there." He strokes her head awaiting a response or some form of recognition, but no words or physical response is uttered. Only the recognisable sounds of a gentle snore.

Joseph gently gets up, allowing Alayna's head to soften against the haystack they were sitting on. He treds towards the campsite, picking up a mallet and helping the men set up camp in the close distance.

He smiles as he too looks to the horizon and watches as his men obtain firewood and put-up field tents, marking ground for temporary fortifications. A knight with a blue tabard approaches carrying his helmet and his face wears a saddened look. It was Jezel.

"Where's the girl?" he whispers.

Joseph points out and looks up to the man. "Over there."

"Then we are at an agreement then?"

Joseph looks concerned. "Yes, yes we are."

The winds ran from the mountains, spiralling and descending, catching the scents of the forest. They bellow down the valley, over the heads of Joseph, Jezel and Alayna and continue across until they head over the hill revealing a country on fire. Smoke rises from the north near the capital, from the castles and the towns.

And as the sun begins to go down, in the distance, a war horn is called and the beating of drums echoes across the valley.

For in this valley death marches, songs of grim and songs of strife as pain envelopes this once noble country as its sons and daughters lay face down in the dirt and its mothers and father mourn for their loss.

22

Sir Osric Erenbell - Orphans and Kings

Inhale. Exhale. Every breath was cold. It was damp from the salt water that smashed against the rocks behind them. A moment's peace, a moment's rest.

Osric and Urg stand with weapons in their hands, staring out into the cold black with furiously flickering torchlight. Both shaking with adrenaline, both sharing that feeling in their stomachs, the same feeling all warriors feel before battle. Fear.

"Let me do the talking."

Urg looks over his right shoulder, staring at Osric who looks towards the approaching mob. "So be it human."

He returns his gaze to join Osric's as four eyes stare out into the night. Four eyes against the dark. Each stands shoulder to shoulder, in perfect alignment they share the same goal and have no differences between their species. Both eager for some form of diplomacy, but ready for the worst.

They then hear another noise from another direction as through the cracks of the forest, three riders appear getting larger and larger as they hurtle towards the pair. They could begin to see them now, two of them bare the mark of the fallen tower on their tabards. They wear heavy chainmail armour and nasal helmets, carrying Lance's and sheathed swords.

The other rider sat atop a large mare with intricate patterns and symbols painted on the horse.

They slowed as they drew near, the larger mare walking towards them with a strut. Osric, however, knew full well who that person was long before they were in sight. The width of him gave him away.

The Baron smiles. He fashioned a fur and velvet red coat, with thick trousers and an intricate fur hat. In his left hand he carries a brown leather bag while his right holds the horse's reins.

"Ah, mighty Sir Osric. You have completed half the task I sent you on! All you need to do now is cut that monster's throat and I'll reward you with riches beyond your wildest dreams!"

Osric does not flinch at the words the Baron just uttered. His eyes continue to glare at him, holding face.

"Your crimes against the laws of Gesantia, the laws of Caldaria and the very foundations that our civilization was built on has not gone unnoticed, your grace."

The Baron licks his lips and looks to the orc.

"Do you understand the common tongue monster? Or do I need to smack rocks against the wall and jump up and down to communicate."

Urg bites his tongue as he grips his axe tighter and bends his knees, setting a further foundation into the snow in readiness to strike a blow.

The Baron's eyes darted between them both, giving a delayed smile.

"So, I have a proposition. Hand yourselves in, and my men will leave your child alone, dear orc."

Urg's eyes open wider as he lowers his axe just so slightly for a split second and stares at him in shock. "How do you know of my boy?"

The Baron's eyes once again flick between them, taunting Osric and then settle to glare at Urg. His grin rips his cheeks apart revealing crow's feet and dimples and his teeth almost pierce their eyes like sharpened stakes.

"Oh, my dear boy. Your wife is a delicate soul."

Urg grips at his stone axe tighter and paces forward while Osric moves in front of him, stopping his advance.

"Where is she? Where have you taken her?"

The Baron flicks his reins to the side, showing his left side to them both.

"She's here, with us. Listening to your pathetic questions."

Urg looks from left to right, frantically trying to spot her while Osric looks to the Baron and then to the ground as he holds Urg back.

"Where? Where human?"

The Baron smiles again and tosses the leather bag.

"Here." The bag sinks into the snow as the head of a female orc rolls out from within.

The Baron smiles, delighted to see the horror on the orc's face.

Urg looks down in shock at first, breathing slow but heavy breaths as he grits his tusks, bulging his veins out to the top of his skin and then screams in defiance.

"ZU ZHATA ZAFRAZZI"

Osric is smashed to the floor as the orc charges towards the Baron with fury in his eyes.

He barrels through the snow watching the two henchmen charge towards him. He leaps forward, with his hands eager to snap his neck. But, alas, he connects with one of the Baron's men who manoeuvres himself in the way.

Urg lands atop of the henchman's shoulder, gripping from his face as the henchman screams from the strength and weight. The orc begins to bite at his neck ripping out the flesh spitting out bloody giblets to the ground, staining the snow a sanguine red.

Osric leaps up, grabbing his sword from the ground and watches as the other henchman gallops at full speed, ramming a lance into Urg's side, shattering his ribs and making him scream in agony while sending spluttered wood everywhere.

"Run Arelle, Run!" Osric turns his head, now looking towards the onslaught.

He charges into the fold, running directly for the Baron. His left-hand clenches his elf tear while his other clenches his sword, gripping it ready to swing at any moment.

Urg pushes the henchman to the ground and watches the Baron gallop off to meet the ever nearer angry mob he had ignited earlier. He adds to their fury with additional poisonous words.

"You see the monster we face! You see him rip the flesh from a man's neck!

Protect your home's and your families! Kill them! Charge!!"

A raised fist, smashes into the air and a cacophony of grunts echoes from the forest as the torches bouncing more violently ever closer towards them all.

The henchman draws his sword and turns towards Osric who makes good ground towards him.

The horse gallops at full speed.

Osric side steps, swinging his sword up from his legs and aims high towards the incoming mare. It was a successful strike as the blade glides through its neck and smashes against the rider's chest, sending him crashing down into the snow as his feet are ripped from their stirrups.

The horse's legs continue to gallop forwards but after a few steps it falls lifeless, crashing down to the ground in a limp fashion, nerve endings giving out delayed gutters as the horse spasms at the impact.

Osric charges over, looking down at the man squirming for his life as his legs are twisted and broken from the fall and his hands are held out to defend himself. But, without hesitation, Osric rams his sword into his chest all the easier, once, twice, thrice. Each scream was more blood curdling than the other.

He looks towards the field, and it is as if the crowd of men were not there, as Urg was hell bent on reaching the Baron. Osric watched the orc rip pieces of loose wood from his chest, while his feet carry him through the snow.

What sounds like a whistling wind can be heard from above. It was slow at first but became louder and louder the more Osric focused on it. He looked up, to see flicks of little dark shadows made clear in the dimness by the torches.

"Urg! Get down!" Osric crouches to the floor, holding his left hand up into the air forcing a blue mirage around him.

Three seconds pass, no more no less than twenty or so arrows slam into the area around him, having bounced off the magical sphere that protected him. Some splinter where the magic was strong, others snap in the fall, a few pierce the ground while others stand proud in the dead henchman.

Osric doesn't think, he only stands back up after the volley and continues pushing forward, rushing through the snow with heavy steps.

The flicker of torchlight from the forest was enough to show the silhouette. An orc on his knees in the snow, with three, maybe four arrows sticking out from his chest.

The orc tries to scream, he tries to shout, he tries to defy. But one of the arrows had pierced through his heart, another through his stomach and lungs, his wounds were too much, even for his kin. Osric catches him before he falls, as the light from his eye is still failing but not given out yet.

"Human"

Blood floods from his mouth as his finger touches Osric's chest and looks up towards his eyes.

"Zafrazzi"

More blood floods, as his lungs give way from the pressure and impact and his eyes roll to the back of his head while his weight gives way. Osric lets him fall to the snow and goes to grasp his sword and elf tear.

He looks up, suddenly aware of his surroundings again, and there he stands, amongst a mass of over one hundred men, with eyes that pierce the veil of darkness that surround them, hungry for more blood, hungry to envelop the world in a sinister shadow and he was the only thing standing in their way.

Exhale, Inhale.

23

Koga - A Sea of Grass

The ground lay scorched and what looked to be the remains of the tall grass in this region was charred and burnt, leaving blackened dirt and ashen rock. The Acea trees swayed with leafless branches, soaking up the sun's rays until sitting as lifeless husks, giving way to premature deaths in this dire heat.

Their journey south started with beautiful plains that had long stretches of savannah grass and blooming buds of flowers. As their steps counted upwards the vibrance of the grass, flowers and trees spiralled downwards as if their footsteps were sapping their life away and the heat from the sun was much more intense.

Many weeks ago, the Zafrazzi chieftain laid a Pride symbol crafted by hand out of Acea wood. It stood proud from the ground to mark the edge of their territory; the chieftain had made a spectacle of erecting it, declaring it as their territorial boundary and announcing a new Pride rule that anyone who was to cross this point without consent would be defying him and breaking Pride promise. At the ceremony, the symbol was striking in contrast to the savannah grass, now it blended into the barren horizon that surrounded it.

Koga looks hesitantly at the symbolic statue, and then looks to Leandro who tallies behind him.

"Leandro, have you packed enough water? We don't know how long we will be, or where this path will take us."

Leandro fluffs some dirt from the ground between his fingers and then smells its complexion. "I did. Good job too. No water in these parts for weeks at least."

Koga restlessly looks behind him from once they come, eyeing up the horizon. "No one followed us, do you think? Maybe we should camp out here before we press on Leandro?"

Leandro looks towards him and quizzes him with his eyes. "I suppose we could rest for a while; the sun will stop hurting our backs soon if it decides to retreat into the lands on the horizon." He looks around and points out a spot of ground with shade covered by a craggy rock that hangs like a giant fang. "There."

The two retire, propping themselves up against the rock, resting for a moment before exhaustion from adrenaline and exertion gives way and their limbs, minds and eyes collapse to sleep. As darkness takes them to the dream land, morphing reality and the passage of time, Koga begins to dream of vivid plays inside his mind.

He stands within a room of black glass, like dreaded marble that eats all the colours it meets. There he watches as Leandro sits atop a throne made of bones. Bones of his kinsman, of orcs and Landari while he smiles with vigour and with hatred. "Koga, look what we have built together! A new Zafrazzi, like the old days of Amukelani. Our songs will be sung, for years to come and our pelts will live with the chiefs of the future."

Koga looks to his hands, which drip blood to the ground, watching it fall beneath the glass and into a void of darkness. "There is no Pride left, Leandro, why do you smile? Why do you snigger? It is not the way our ancestors would have wanted our futures?"

Leandro stands, holding a blade within his hand that drips shadowy ichor and walks forwards towards Koga. "You disrespect me Zaffaza? You disrespect my values and my teachings? How do you know what our ancestors did? How do you judge me and my way? My Pride? My Zafrazzi?"

Koga draws his axe with his bloody hands.

"I am not a Zaffaza, you are the one without Pride."

He breaths deep.

"Zu Zhata Zafrazzi!"

He charges forwards, through the black glass that now begins to grow tendrils that grip at his ankles. He leaps, holding his axe above his head before swinging it at the approaching Leandro.

Their weapons collide, shattering the stone into flint-like splinters. Koga cries loudly, to the heavens and looks to his arm. It was broken.

"You are not a Zaffaza." Leandro reels the blade to his side. "You are nothing."

He thrusts, catching Koga in the centre chest, smothering him in a black smoke that envelops his body and enters into every orifice it could, through his skin, his ears and eventually his eyes.

Koga woke from his nightmare, shaking and sweating with anxiety startling Leandro who lay next to him. "Brother? Are you okay? Are you having visions from the dreamland again?"

Koga wipes the sweat from his brow and stands up. "Yes, but it is nothing."

He pauses and then looks over to Leandro. "I'm uncomfortable about going forward."

His friend nods and stands up with him and face to face they stare at each other. Visually so different, yet the same pride, bound in history and ritual.

"Nerves are good. Nerves will make your step faster and your victory ever more sweet."

Leandro slaps his shoulder. Listening and assuming without asking why.

"Come on, we always talked about going south, I will make the breach and you can follow." He drags a slow long intake of water, adjusts his pack, readying himself for the journey ahead. He slaps Koga on the shoulder again and makes haste, almost like a child playing tag. He passes the Pride symbol and without stopping glances back at Koga, not even contemplating that he wouldn't follow. He was right of course; he always could influence him.

They continue their journey and time passes along the rocky crags and rough plains. Each sees the same landscape to the horizon, a scarred mess of rocks and light brown dirt that covers the plain, sinking into itself like a barren waste. Yet, their journeys within are very different.

"Two days of travel, and nothing Leandro. Only rocks and death." Koga kicks a loose stone on the floor. It flies through the air, catching the wind before falling into a crater a few yards away.

"We should turn back and look somewhere else; at this rate we will find nothing out here and you know it's disrespectful to return with no food to add to the feast of the great hunt."

Leandro looks to the horizon through the haze. He squints, catching whatever glimpse of life he can. "If we turn back now, we forfeit our chance to succeed Koga. We will lose our only chance to break the mould and become legend."

Leandro looks back at him. But Koga looks in the distance, passing thought strikes against Leandro's mind.

'Was their brotherhood torn here he thought. Was their brotherhood nothing? If he didn't follow me into this life, then what is the point of him being here.'

On the horizon, smoke begins to pump its way into the sky, distinguishable between the haze. Even though Koga wasn't in the best of spirits about the entire situation, he manages to raise a smile at the first sight of prey and shares a knowing glance with Leandro, melting into the moment.

"Minos maybe?"

Leandro raises his snout and begins sniffing the air. "Possibly. They are not cooking meat that's for sure." He pauses before drawing his stone axe. "Come, let's see if we can earn our pride."

The two begin walking through the scorched lands, down through the banks of light brown soil and up an embankment of rocky crags. The landscape held no rodents, no insects and no predators. The occasional acea tree sparks interest, but again, the roots are null and its bark dry giving only a memory of the beauty that these lands once were.

The smoke plumed out from beyond the hilltop, as the two began the slight ascension to view who or what lurked below. As they came closer, they lay down in the dirt, crawling, edging slowly up the embankment to view and confirm the assumption of Minos. There were three Minos having a discussion around a campfire. However, their attention was not on the Minos and their camp, but instead, beyond the rolling barrens, their eyes met a sight of unnatural beauty.

A beautiful lapis crystal display refracted from a craterous formation that seemed to regurgitate out from the belly of the world. It was about two miles ahead yet illuminated the sky as the crystals cast beautiful rainbow lights beneath the rays of the sun... They could see a hazy cloud of dust pump into the atmosphere above, adding to the plume that choked the sky. Many thoughts crossed through their minds, as they played out assumptions of its material. Although they both knew it was magic, they could feel it hitting their lungs and nostrils. A powerful magic to reach them this far out.

It was most likely a raw vein of elven tear, the sparse land and sun ripping up the soil enough to expose it to elements. That would explain the oasis in the barren plain. Legend is that at the foot of a raw eleven tear vein life thrives - no one knows why whether magic or nutrients. At the crater ahead life was thriving, with rolling green grass, beautiful orchards of what appeared to be fruit trees and rivers of crystal-clear water.

"What is this place?" Koga looks to Leandro as his mind fills with questions.

He hesitates at first, looking down towards the Minos feasting on food from the fire. "I'm not sure, but this is why we are here. This will explain many things, Koga, many things."

Koga remains puzzled.

"Leandro, they are Minos! Passing the symbol is one thing but you know we are at peace with Minos. Why are we trying to break what the chieftain has been working on trying to build for so many years now?"

Leandro snaps his head towards him. "Have you heard yourself Koga? Have you heard the words that have come out of your mouth? You sound like a coward? Are you not meant to be my brother? Zu Zhata Zafrazzi? We have talked until the sun has gone down and risen again of our heritage, our Pride. I don't understand why you question me, and now of all times?"

The orc listens with concern. "I'm sorry brother, I didn't mean to disrespect you."

Leandro lifts his axe up from his sash and looks to Leandro. "Then let us get to work."

He leaps to his feet and snarls at his prey before screaming at the top of his lungs.

"ZU ZHATA ZAFRAZZI"

The three Minos startled and scurried in an attempt to grab at their weapons, which are loosely scattered around the encampment. As they run, you can see they are wide, have broad shoulders and heavy backs and stand at around eight foot tall. To Leandro, they look like athletic rhinos, slender and built for speed and power.

Leandro slams down to the ground like a coiled spring and swiftly releases his stone axe into the air towards one of the Minos. One of the Minos is part way picking up his spear, when the axe connects to his face and sends him grovelling to the ground.

Koga looks on, watching his brother react so swiftly and he charges forward himself, axe in hand as he parades down the red stoned embankment towards the camp. Leandro leaps forward again, aiming to mount the Minos' back. He connects using the axe as leverage and his claws as anchors. He yanks the axe from the Minos' face, sending it into a fit of rage; he acts swiftly and skilfully, slamming the axe into the Minos' chest.

The orc is fast approaching the camp, carefully assessing and analysing the whereabouts of the Minos and his brother. He watches as one of the Minos arms himself and crouches low, aiming his spear towards him. Koga reacts, sidestepping to the left and smashing the spear with his axe to the side. The failed attempt angers the Mino who screams as he charges forward, abandoning his spear to the ground as he uses his hands to try and grapple Koga. He is no match, far too slow in comparison to the orc, who slams his axe into its chest.

He leaves no room for retribution using all of his weight as he pushes deeper into the cavity, winding the Minos. He pulls the axe back and cleaves again which is right on target this time, breaking through the skin and hitting his heart. The blood erupts immediately, pulsing like a volcano as the heart continues to pump, it flows onto the barren land which willingly accepts the moisture leaving a stain rather than a puddle where it settles.

Leandro looks around, watching his brother finish off the second Minos. It all happened so quickly the third is still searching for his weapon, frantically throwing pieces of camping equipment into the field as he looks over his shoulder.

Leandro grins, as he manoeuvres himself closer to the creature wiping his axe on his loincloth. The scared Minos gives up his search, stands up straight and hastily begins to climb up the embankment, looking behind him with every step he can muster.

Leandro follows, bolting up the hill.

"Koga! Flank him!"

The two-give chase, watching the Minos climb up the embankment and then over the ridge.

Leandro follows, moments away from casting his axe into his leg but as he steps atop the hill, looking down on the descending ridge, he sees the Minos has slid down, gaining enough space between them to not warrant a chase, the Minos know their lands well, and had the upper hand.

"Koga." Leandro turns around to find him, as he pants with a heavy breath. "Koga!"

"Yes brother?" They meet amongst the two dead Minos.

"Are you wounded?"

Koga looks down at himself, wiping and dusting off the grimness of battle. "Fine, no scratches."

"Good. Good."

They look down at the two Minos' carcasses on the floor, and Leandro bends down with his weapon at one of their faces.

"The horns will be enough as a trophy Koga, go, take yours."

He points over towards the other carcass before using his axe to butcher the horns from his kills face. But, Koga watches hesitantly. He watches his brother begin the procedure feeling disgust, guilt and remorse that they have broken two rules. They couldn't take this one back, it was not a meal, and not only could it jeopardise their lives and make them Zaffaza, but it could also start a war.

But then again, maybe Leandro was right. Maybe this was the right way to approach things. Maybe this was the step forward towards the true Zafrazzi. He shakes his head and walks towards his kill.

No matter, it's only two Minos? That won't hurt. Will it? He thought

24

Sir Osric Erenbell - The Cry to the Crossroads

"Sir Osric. My dear, dear friend. Far too much blood has been spilt today. The field runs red already." The shadow of the Baron looms at the edge of the forest's edge, licking the air with his tongue.

Osric stands with his arms open nearly shoulder width apart, elf tear in one hand and a sword in the other. His eyes look down to Urg's body before looking up to the crowd of men.

"You all have a choice." He exhales.

"You have a choice today to despise tyranny and shun it in the face. For so long you have lived secluded and clueless to the world outside. A better world, an equal world. Where all genders and races live in harmony."

The crowd looks onward. Void of reaction, of physical movement or even thought.

"No, my dear, dear Sir Osric. I think you remain unclear. You are the one contained in tyranny. Like a fly caught in a web. For it is you who must make a choice."

The Baron's horse trots over, and a fat sausage hand reaches out into the dark. "Come, lay down your arms and I will spare your life and throw you in my dungeon until you have reflected on your decision and your thoughts…"

A delayed grin wreaks havoc across the Baron's face, smirking like a child that has swiped a couple of cakes from a freshly baked tray while it cools. Osric stares at him seeing through the smirk, a void, absent of thought, empty of emotion.

"Your daughter does not want anything to do with this regime. Your tyranny ends here. I give you and your men the choice as well."

He raises his voice for all to hear, stepping out from his defensive position and looking towards the twisted crowd bewitched by the poisonous words and evil actions of the Baron.

"You answer to no one other than yourself. You are bound by the laws of Gesantia and in those laws you have a say in its politics. I say, today you make the choice to stand down, give your weapons to the snow and return to your homes."

The crowd begins to chuckle, a small little chuckle that crescendos into a full blown belly laugh peppered with shouting slanderous comments, evil remarks and curses. Osric watches on, staring at the crowd who almost react like a hive, like a swarm of pests.

"Then I bid you a safe journey on the paths ahead and that the roads you pick lead you to the Well Wood trees. May the afterlife be kinder to you than the death you choose."

The Baron claps his hands as he spits to the ground and gallops his horse towards the men. "Bring him alive! I want him to answer for his crimes!"

A horn sounds and so begins the charge through the snow, unranked, undisciplined, frightened peasants working themselves into a fury with promises of a 'better world'. Pitchforks and ploughs, staves and old weapons. Ill equipped and unprepared but equally matched with motivation, drive and willingness to make the ultimate sacrifice.

Osric side-steps to the right and slams his elf tear into his leg. A blue shimmer emanates from within, and a cloud of blue light smothers his body with a haze. The crowd continues to charge, some faster than others as the young are eager to claim the glory. Osric begins his advance forward as the first young boy tries to swing his axe into his left side, attempting to end this battle swiftly. But Osric raises the elf tear into the air, meeting the attacker before contact.

The boy's chest cavity caves in, snapping and crushing sounds break from within his torso as a force of magic pushes against him, sending him flying into the air and smashing into a tree some way off in the distance. The tree sways, unleashing a pile of settled snow from its leaves. Osric raises the tear once more, reinvigorating the force field around him.

Another young man hot on the heels of the first approaches from the right. He thrusts his pitchfork at Osric, connecting with the blue haze that still remains. A rush of colour leaves Osric and travels up sending a shockwave of light up the weapons shaft and into the boy's hands erupting his bones into fragments and leaving his hands a singeing mess. Osric cascades his longsword into the man's stomach emptying the contents onto the floor. The boy screams, grabbing at his entrails with his stumps to put them back in, crying in agony.

The onslaught continues as hordes of men begin to scream into the air resisting their very nature, swinging their weapons frantically trying to rally themselves. They continue coming one by one, rapidly ever more eager like a pack of dogs on a hunt. Each one is easier for Osric to destroy than the one before as his power intensifies like the heat of a fire while the slaughter continues.

A surge of intense power is building within Osric; he can feel it coming, pre-empting a surge he charges into the ranks surrounding himself with the men who try and defile him. He swings his sword with skill, erupting the crowd into a dance of woe. The blade cleaves through the flesh and bone as the men of Rookeries Rest try their hardest to fight, to resist death but fail. Some route with lost limbs, grasping tightly at their cleaved arms and legs. Others lay dead on the cold floor with their blood adding to the world.

The Baron looks on, watching it all play out, with a fury in his eyes and he begins to grit at his teeth. The battle enrages in front of him as he sits atop of his horse looking down upon them in a haze. "Retreat! Retreat my men! The man is possessed by a demon! This that is where his power comes from!"

The men rejoice over the order, they retreat, some running back, some hopping, others crawling. It's a stampede of the able, who gather, panting as they stand behind the Baron, who holds out his hands and yields. Those that were wounded, unable to walk, had outstretched their hands reaching and hoping for comrades to aid them to safety. They were ignored, long term friends and neighbours, disregarded and trodden into the snow. It was a sorry sight with many moaning, harrowing cries of those left to die, with the hungry murder of crows gathering.

"Many have died that didn't have to."

A blade pries loose from the skull of a fallen fletcher who still crawls as the end of his nerves give off their last moments before flickering to nothingness.

Osric looks to the Baron. "Your attempts to poison the world in filth will not go unpunished. Xanathose has been made aware and your time as a free man in this world is drawing to a close."

The Baron dismounts his horse, into the blue vapour that hangs in air and his eyes wander towards Osric. At first, a sense of confusion runs across his face but then realisation begins to sink in. "Please……"

He falls to the floor laying in the snow grovelling like a leper in the street.

"Please." He looks up to him, grasping at his hands and praying." You don't understand. I'm sick. I'm sick. I must see a surgeon of the mind. Terrible things pass through my head."

Osric stares down at him, cold and hopeless but with an essence of concern and watches as the Baron begins to grasp at his head.

"I need to talk to you about something. Please, plea…."

He begins to jitter, as his head swiftly snaps in an almost fit-like state. Osric looks on at this grim display and begins to cast a shadow of doubt.

"Go home." He looks to those of Rookeries Rest, the ones who are wounded, the ones who valiantly tried to best one of Caldaria's greatest warriors but were met with failure. Osric turns, sheathing his bloody sword while continuing to hold onto his glowing elf tear that emanates power.

The Baron begins choking, as his nose bleeds and he heaves from his stomach and vomits blood from his mouth. Osric ignores him as he walks through the snow, shepherding the men back from where they'd come from.

Now the battle has recessed, he can hear the crying of a baby from the boats bobbing on the water. He is confused, they should have left, why haven't they left. He reacts at once, charging forward as he makes his way through the icy ground, thrusting his legs through as he pushes against the easterly winds and hailing weather. Arelle is seen sifting through other small wooden boats, throwing bits of rope and fishing net out from within.

"What are you doing? Why haven't you left?"

Arelle turns, drawing out a knife from her pouch before bursting into tears as she sees Osric.

"I can't find a second oar. There isn't one anywhere." She drops the dagger.

"Get back in the boat, I will see if I can find one."

She nods, darting back across the wooden decks of the harbour and into the small boat bobbing about. The orc baby cries softly.

"Start pushing off, I will catch up."

Osric makes his way to the nearby fishing hut, inside a net hangs from the ceiling with many hooks and appendages. There, stacked in the corner were plenty of oars to choose from. He grabs one, making his way outside before tossing the oar to Arelle.

He jumps into the freezing water and the ripples slam against his knees as he grasps hold of the boat with his left hand. Using his right, he puts his sword into the boat and then holds the elf tear, giving off a bright light to guide the way which also lets down the energy that was acting as a defence for him in battle.

He pushes forward, shivering as the water creeps up his body towards his waist before stopping the boat in front of him as he prepares to enter.

"We are safe now, let's just get out of the bay."

Arelle comforts the baby and smiles a teary face towards Osric while they both share a moment of calm.

He smiles at her and before lifting his legs to get out of the water, he stops.

A bite. A bite in his back. One which was hollow but deep. One that stopped his breath that remained heavy against his plate armour. His elf tear fell, sinking into the depths below, still glowing a rush of power, shining his face. He pushes against the boat, letting the current take it, fighting the waves with each step. The raised banners of the broken town, marching out of he forest and onto the beach, loading up their crossbows as Osric peers behind him.

"Osric? What's wrong? What's wrong?" Her hand, reaching out to his, digging her nails into his skin.

He bites down, spitting out a fresh spew of blood, turning his head to the boat again and then looking to Arelle.

"Row."

Her eyes fix with his, shocked.

"No, Osric. No I can't leave you here. Yo..."

"You... must... row."

His words heavy. His body, tired. His skin cold.

Another bite, this time at his right shoulder, crushing the steel plate that protects it and making its home inside his flesh.

"Row...."

The words tire as he shuffled through the water, now heavier than ever. His left arm held out, grasping the boat as he pushes all his weight and force against it.

The oars cast into the water, now breaking the current as Arelle uses all her might to push forwards. She leans against Jay, shielding him from the flurry of bolts that fire from the beach.

The Ocean in front of her, smothered in a cold mist.

And then, a third bolt strikes. Just under his gorget. Just deep enough to pierce his spine and rip the nerve endings connecting to his head.

He collapses into the drink below, sinking as the water begins to fill between the crevices of his armour. His vision begins to blur behind the rippled brine, but his eyes remain fixed onto the boat. Each cast of the oars can be seen, sending a disturbance and ripple of waves against the current. Each successful stroke in rhythm to his own heartbeat.

Row.... Row..... Row

The pain did not take presidence in his mind, as in a spur of hopelessness, he chants to himself. Hoping for Arelle and Jay to at least make it out of the bay alive.

Bolts pepper the water above him and as they do, they stop, floating down towards the ocean floor below, gilded within the light of the blue light from the tear. Like little rain drops running down a cold glass frame.

The boat still pushes through the water, bumping against the waves, still in rhythm with the beat of his heart, still in time with the chants in his mind.

Row..... Row.......Row.....

Until, the darkness took him. Until it added another soul to its roster.

25

Koga - Beyond the World of Magic

As is often the way, finding the way home was much easier than the outward path, even with the extra weight - supplies gathered from the camp and cuts from their hunt. Although sharing the same journey, the experiences of the comrades along the way couldn't have been more divergent. Koga was troubled. His mind was terrorising him, returning each time they rested to his walks in the dreamlands, the dream repeating and worsening like a festering wound. It filled his mind all day and night, while Leandro grew increasingly triumphant and elated. Their venture into the unknown had reaped rewards; his imagination raced ahead playing out their return. His companionship is limited to fantasy storytelling of their return, with little notice of Koga's well-being. How their contribution and trophies they carry will be far beyond anything else the others will offer to the table. The horns of the Minos from the great tribes to the south untamed lands.

He would declare to the chieftain a return to the old ways, to the tribe that their ancestors built all those years ago. The tribe would support him as so many spoke it, aligning with Leandro's hallowing thoughts that their current chieftain spent his entire life seeking peace. There was no reason or purpose other than to fatten himself up and live like a King from across the sea.

The Savannah grass blew in the hot wind, whisking up pieces of yellow grass seed and blowing it into the air. It flutters alongside a thin stream of water that trickles through an encampment of leather and bone tents that numerously line the plains.

"Leandro…"

The Landari turns to Koga. "I fear we will be made Zaffaza today… I fear it and almost know it deep down. The chieftain will punish us for this."

Leandro smiles. "I would like to see him try."

Leandro walks in with a lifted chin and an excited smile, but Koga anxiety grows and grows intensifying with every step that brings them closer to home. "Koga!" A flurry of young children charges over to the two of them.

"Hey kids. You should all be hunting!" He laughs

"You always say that. You bet we would if we could Koga. The elders say we are too young."

Leandro watches as Koga crouches down to them. He scruffs a young Landarian girl's hair and embraces them all with a hug.

"I love you kids, I really do." His mood momentarily lifted with the children. He looks over to Leandro, pensively.

"If we don't take partners Leandro. If we don't find our bonded spirits in this life. Will you take residence with me? We can raise children to be great warriors. Maybe that's what we could do with our lives?"

Leandro grins, nodding his head, staring at the children tugging at Koga's hair. The orc stands up, with one of the children sitting atop his shoulder. But deep down, Leandro wanted more of a life than that, he wanted dominion of the plains, to be a mighty chieftain and today he would make a start.

"We shouldn't delay. Best get our offering to the chief before daylight leaves the sky." The two continue through the yurt fields and tented homes, looking at the marvellous culture that they represent while the children gather around them, play fighting amongst each other.

There from the distance, a party of Zafrazzi walk through the streets with bloodied weapons and skinned animal coats. A great orc is amongst them, wearing armour of bone, as he rides atop a giant hyena. The creature, dripping pools of saliva from its hungry mouth, turns its head towards them. It releases a delighted cackle as it sees them both, with dried blood upon its chops.

"Boys! How did the hunt go?" The orc slaps the creature's back and strokes its mane, then throws it some chewing fat to enjoy while it waits for another meal it longs for. The creature catches it between its teeth, happy to invest its waiting time with a little snack, while looking towards Koga and Leandro. The two look blankly at the orc and then each other. Before Koga could speak, Leandro lifts up the horn of one of the Minos. "I think we will sit with the chief this year."

The orc atop the hyena-like creature stares at first, puzzled and slightly confused but then looks at them concerned.

"And what exactly is that? Digging in the ground finding creatures of the past? or scavenging the scraps that the pridelands have to offer? That will not fetch you a boon from the chief, young Zafrazzi."

Koga sinks into his feet, eyes casting their way towards the horn and then to Leandro who smiles and nods."

"Minos."

"You do understand that what you have done is against the rules and forbidden?" His gaze turns to the large hut in the centre of the encampment made of the bones and remains of a winged lizard that once drew fire from its belly.

Amukelani the Dread claimed the dragon's soul for the Pride, slaughtering it alone and then dining on its flesh. All warriors claim to be him in reincarnation and all children strive to be like him as adults for his embodiment of the Zafrazzi Zatessi. The Pride King.

The hut adorned the skins and tusks of all the fallen members of the Pride, all those who gave their lifeblood for the Zafrazzi. Made into pelts and chimes that dangle from the ceiling so that their songs can be remembered forever, they hang like messages from a vine, each with their own story to be told.

"The chief will want to hear an explanation from you, I suggest you ready your excuses now."

Leandro and Koga look at each other, giving out faces in equal measure, one of frustration and anger, the other of anxiety and fear. Leandro is the first to avert his gaze back to the large orc. "No excuses, only pride." Leandro growls, pushing past the hyena as he begins his walk through the dirt paths.

Koga lets the child down. "What was that about Leandro, we could have sold the story to him? He may have supported us?" Leandro snaps as he turns around and roars thunder in Koga's face.

"We do not gain idle support from cowards. Those who support the chieftain in his regime are not Zafrazzi." Koga stands back, staring at the dust like a scalded schoolboy.

"We are not part of this new Pride that the chieftain is trying to ram into our throats. We are part of the true Zafrazzi. Koga we are better than that. We are like our ancestors." Leandro kicks off, charging towards the hut as he un-attaches the horn from his belt, Koga follows, staggering behind trying to keep up with the dust trail Leandro had made from his haste.

"Leandro! Wait! Let us approach with caution! Yo...."

Leandro turns with a fire in his heart. "Caution? Why should I be cautious with such a story to be told? I am going over there now and I'm going to show my kill with pride and then make history, dear brother...."

Leandro bursts into the hut, holding out the horn of the Minos in his hands and growls. Inside was a firepit which burnt old sticks of lavender and acea wood in its pit. Atop the stove sits an ancient cauldron from which the smell of bubbling spices and herbs fill the room, enticing the noses of those around them.

"You enter into this sacred tent with the bones of another without being invited? Do you not know your sacred vows, Lion?" An elderly Landari stands, springing to his feet. His mane was grey and messy but had bones of his past conquests on show, dangling from it. He looks towards the horn that is held in Leandro's hand and a shock falls across his face.

"You disobey me? And you burst in uninvited?"

"But I was invited, this hall has always been a public space. It has always been a place of union of Pride and protection." He points his claw snarling as he does. "But you changed that."

The chieftain shakes his head walking towards Leandro with concern in his breath. "My Pride, my hall, my rules. If I want you to leave, I will. I am the Chief, and you are just another runt struck on power."

Leandro roars as he begins to charge, but Koga steps in front, pulling him to one side.

"What was your plan of action? You cannot just barge in here, it's sacred. You cannot just attack him without declaring Zatazzi. A claim for power like this will not go unpunished and you will be mocked!" Koga hurriedly whispers

Leandro laughs and speaks for all to hear. "This is not sacred ground, this is Zafrazzi ground, the ground of the Pride. The land of the free and the wishful. Restricting your people from entering Zafrazzi ground is not your decision to make."

The old lion laughs as he walks towards Leandro, grinning an impressive set of teeth under his mouth. "If you knew what I know, if you knew about the world, about the plains, about the lands beyond the sea. You would do the same. We live in a dark time and a dark world, one filled with mysteries that leave our origin to no answers."

Leandro smiles. "So you're a coward?" Koga again tries to push Leandro aside but is greeted with forceful anger and is instead pushed away. Koga watches on, hopeless to the outcome of Leandro's stubborn mind.

"What did you just call me?" The old lion watches them both.

"You're a coward for letting our people be slaves to peace. Why do you not let them hunt? Why do you not let them fight the Minos?" says Leandro angrily as he flickers between the eyes of the old lion and his guards.

The chieftain looks down towards the horn of the Minos on display, no longer dripping blood after being 2 days old. "Narmenia, Zakia, I want these two bound and put to trial now!"

Leandro laughs. "Bind and trial us? When the people hear of my proposal, the Pride will flock to me to lead."

The two large orcs grab hold of them both, tying rope around their arms. Koga resists at first, slumping his back and pushing the restraints away with his shoulders but after hearing Leandro's voice, he struggles less, allowing the men to bind him.

"Brother, this will only show his treachery more. We know that." Koga listens as he struggles no more.

"Good. Your choice will be easy." The chieftain pauses then gives them the ultimate choice, passing the motion that no Pride member wants to hear "Death or Zaffaza?"

Koga jolts at the motion, scrunching his face, looking concerningly at Leandro. "This is what I feared, brother. This is what we spoke of."

Leandro looks across to him from the corner of his eyes. "The treachery is his, brother. That is why he gives us the choice to be exiled or killed."

The old lion snarls, snapping his jaws with his teeth. "Quiet fools. I will give you the choice to die and go to the plains or to live your life without Pride. I suggest you pick the first option. Maybe you will come back to us as someone far less defiant."

He pushes one of the orcs with his large palms. "Gag them and take them to the Zentnee, once your there sound the gong. The Pride will decide if my judgement is fitting."

"Yes chief." The two orcs nod, grunting as they wrap leather bindings around Leandro's snout and stuff Koga's mouth full of linen. They begin pushing Leandro and Koga through the streets, as passers-by watch them thrown to the ground like dogs.

"Get up, worms." Zakia lifts his leg, kicking Leandro in the back and laughing. They continue through the streets as the Pride watch and look towards them.

"Zaffaza!" A sum of vegetables are thrown towards them, smacking against their faces and as they do the rest of the crowd joins in with screaming abuse becoming louder.

"Leandro? Koga? I thought they were good Zafrazzi?"

The crowd gathers more, and their chants become louder.

"I hope you walk through the desert and lose your soul!"

"Defiant! Zaffaza!"

The names are called as they are pushed through the trodden paths towards a purposeful open area. The ground here is littered with dried bones from the hot sun, picked clean from the previous hunt or from scavengers. It paves the ground until there is a pedestal and platform of acea wood and leather bindings with a gong sitting atop.

"Into the Zentnee. Moving out of the circle is forbidden until you are invited out, defilers." The orcs kick them in, watching as they land on the bones which snap under their weight. Crunching and snapping sounds fill the air before dispersing into the wind as quickly as they are made.

Leandro lifts his chest up, looking over to Koga. "Brother."

But Koga's eyes do not meet his, for they still look to the bones on the floor, the brittle bleached bones from the sun that line it. "Do not call me that."

A shocked face warms the lion while his heart jolts against his chest with adrenaline. "But I don't understand?"

Koga looks to him with a pain in his eyes, grinding his tusks as he does. The orc bolts, from his crouched position and pins Leandro to the Ground. "You didn't have a plan? You went in blind on raw emotion. At what point was that a good idea? At what point did you think you would succeed?"

Leandro does not speak or struggle, he remains frozen in shock.

"You are not fit to be chief. You don't listen. You would only take the Pride to their death. I see you in my visions in the dreamlands. I see you on a throne of bones as you feast upon the corpses of the Zafrazzi. You are no ruler; you are not fit for the future of our tribe. And if I am to stand against you, I will."

The words cascade into Leandro's ears breaking his sanity as he pushes the orc off him, pinning him to the ground and roaring in his face. But Koga does not flinch. "You are not my brother.... You are dead to me."

The gong sounds and Leandro lifts from him to find that people had already gathered and were enjoying the commotion. Koga lifts up, looking towards the old lion who walks onto the acea wood alone in ceremonial robes, staring down at them both. The Robes were covered with the pelt of what people say is the head of Amukelani, the dread and the tusks of his three orc brothers.

"These two Zafrazzi, have defiled our sacred grounds, have defiled our traditions and have broken a treaty in which I have worked so hard to make."

Leandro growls, snapping his jaws as he stares directly on, but Koga sits with very little thought or expression on his face.

"I was going to give them the choice. To die a Zafrazzi or to live their life without Pride." He addresses the crowd, then pauses, sinking his eyes into both of them.

"Instead, we will let tradition decide. Those who die without fighting will be reborn as runts. Those who die fighting will go to the plains and live their lives in the great hunt forever." The chief paces, creaking across the acea wood and onto the solid earth, the crowds gazing on in anticipation to hear what he had decided.

"One of you will kill the other, and the one who lives will walk with Pride again, unless I deem your fighting unworthy."

The chief smiles a wry smile, delighted at his penalty and looks to the rest of the pride as if in hope that these two will make a good example to them, circling Leandro and Koga as he does.

"So, Zafrazzi, do you accept? Or would you prefer the life of a Zaffaza?"

Leandro looks over to the chief, with shock in his brow, but as he turns to Koga, the orc stands.

"I cannot let you win." Koga breathes heavily. "You will lead the Pride into death and destruction. You act on impulse and will carry weapons that should not be allowed in our world…."

Leandro stands up, with worry over his face. "Brother, I am sorry."

Koga ignores his words and instead screams. "ZU ZHATA ZAFRAZZI" He charges at Leandro, crushing the bones from beneath his feet, with his arms ready to strike him with his brute strength as a weapon.

Leandro stands ready to brace the impact, and as the two connect splinters fly from the ground, as shattered bones fill the air and blood begins to pour from each other's arms and legs and feet.

The crowd looks on, not making noises, not chanting or booing. But watching two Zafrazzi win back their Pride. The notable reaction was from the chieftain who grins, slipping into the crowds while keeping a watchful eye on the two warriors fighting for more than their lives. His eyes seem to grace Leandro more than Koga. Was it a coincidence?

26

Lady Alayna Astravix - A Kingdom Fit for a Queen

Days pass into night. Night passes into day and before the week begins, a new one comes around the corner. Once the moon graced in full but came and went. And on the mark of the second moon, in the light of the new day, a group of horsemen escorting a hay stacked cart, arrive at the foot of the greatest city that ever graced Caldaria. Astronozia, the city at the end of the long road.

The site to behold was far beyond any comparison and for any onlooker, it was easy to assume that the elves constructed it with the help of magic for any normal mason or architect would struggle to even dream of its stature. The walls stood in three layers with the first standing at 20 feet high and at eight foot deep. Towers run across it with ballista and onager acting as the first line of defence against the desperate attackers. It was lined with constant guards well equipped and disciplined.

The second set of walls stood behind a moat of water, which was wide and deep enough to allow trade and transportation travel around the city gates and coordinate the vast city landscape. The walls that stand behind the moat are 300 foot high and 100 foot deep, with towers that bear trebuchets.

The last set of walls stood at the highest, dwarfing the other two and stood immediately behind the second set interconnecting with each other. The wall was a staggering 600 foot high and 240 foot deep, with alcoves so big and so grande that some guardsmen eat, sleep, live and work there without touching solid ground for months and sometimes years.

Great towers network along the last wall housing giant balls of arcane energy that still bear signs of magical properties even to this day. They could catch bolts of lightning to fill up the power reserves which are used to light arcane crystals around the city which guide residence during prolonged periods of darkness. During some months, the walls are so large that when the sun is low towards the morning and late afternoon, or when the winter rains begin, parts of the city are covered in complete darkness that not even the grass grows, drawing lines of gloom to the slums and merchant districts.

But, even then when looking on the horizon, a great spire can be seen from the centre of the city. The central hub of politics and the brain of the community was a 1000-foot-high spire that touched the clouds edge. Atop its peak was another arcane sphere bigger than its counterparts, some three times the size.

The city is so large that it in fact runs across two continents with the largest constructed bridge in existence, high enough and wide enough for great voyaging vessels to pass underneath and for armies to traverse to and from each part. It was almost matched in every way on the other continent with another tower for the faith on the other side.

Alayna sat atop Joseph's mare with him, as she overlooks the city in awe. Her face was still covered in ash and dirt and soot, but her jaw was open so much.

"Your… you're the Prince of this?"

Joseph strokes her shoulder. "Yup, it will be all mine one day. It's not an easy job. Many weeks I go without seeing my father. Sometimes he's still in the city but miles away in the second heart. And when he's not there I take up some of the regal duties."

Alayna looks back towards him, twitching with sexual tension as her skin tickles against his. "What do you mean?"

He looks down at her, brushing her hair from his face. "Two hearts beat for the city of Astronozia. One for the crown and its people, the other for the high bishop and his flock."

A slight pause as he looks over to the great gatehouse. Alayna followed his gaze wondering what had distracted him; the gatehouse dwarfed any fortification buildings Alayna had seen.

"It's my home and it can be your home too. If you'd like?"

Alayna looks up to Joseph as his gaze falls back to her and she remembers a little conversation she had with Martha all those weeks ago. When she said, 'You will make an excellent Queen'.

She thought on and wondered if maybe, just maybe, this is her shot at proving Martha right. Martha would say she was daydreaming too much, not living in the moment and escaping into her imagination. She missed her.

"Yes, I'd like that." She replies, grounding herself in now. The horse trots through the first gate at the first wall and walks along the paved iron road that lines the green well-kept grass at the mouth of the city. In the courtyards left and right, soldiers with heavy armour, large square shields and short swords spar with each other or are seen running in full kit around the grass.

Alayna's eyes quickly glance over towards someone standing at the gatehouse. It was a lovely young woman who beamed a huge smile across her face as she saw them approaching. She has beautifully kept curly black hair with tanned olive skin, and looked ethereal wearing a flowy white gown and loose fitting coat. She was adorned in golden jewels and emerald rings.

"By the gods you've found yourself a pretty bride Joseph? She's lovely!"

Joseph blushes.

"Now now big sister, Alayna has been through a terrible time on her choosing day and nothing was agreed. I entrust her to your care as a dignitary and guest."

Joseph's sister smiles, holding her hand over her mouth to chuckle to herself before lifting it in front of Alayna.

"My name is Katrina! Come! Come! I bet you're in need of a bath and some decent food! I'll have the kitchen make us up some lunch."

Alayna shyly hands out her hand and looks to Joseph before readying herself to dismount the horse, carefully manoeuvring along the stirrup before jumping off and landing sluggishly to the ground.

"I'll see you at dinner butterfly, Katrina will find some clothes that you will fit in, I'm sure!"

Katrina grabs her hand and they both walk through the gatehouse and out of sight.

Joseph remains as he sits on the horse looking up at the magnificent stonework and masonry.

"You're late." A regal voice snaps at the air, but no one else's ears hear them.

"I had an errand to run, I'm sure you heard the news."

"That I did. I also heard you brought in a Gesantian girl?"

Joseph looks to the air, cursing under his lips.

"Lady Alayna Astravix, a distant niece of the Queen of Gesantia…"

"Well… I'd like to meet her, and then we can discuss our plans going forward?"

There is a pause between the mental conversation.

"Yes father, she will, I will let the kitchen staff know you will be making an attendance."

"Good. Godspeed son."

Joseph takes a final look at the gatehouse, before he begins the long road ahead to the spire.

27

Leandro Firemane - The In-Between

Night settled on the plains, shadowing the landscape in a light haze. The light from the two moons dazzled the ground, yet its gaze was weak as the clouds sucked it dry of any purity.

In the day the sky was almost clear but, in the night, the sky was hard to see through the clouds of smoke that strangled the world. In their culture, the Zafrazzi, have never seen stars before, it was a legend, maybe even a myth. Only darkness lived in the night.

While all were asleep, adventuring in the dreamlands, a single soul wanders through the Zafrazzi camp, making sure to tread lightly and very carefully to leave no trace.

"Come quick, inside." The flap of a hut opens, and aromas of incense and blood pour out.

The shadow enters and the head of a lioness peeks out, making sure nothing or no-one is looming around the corner. "Were you followed?"

The Landari sits and hoods himself as he pours little drops of water from his waterskin into his mouth, patting at it to loosen any droplets from the bottom. "No, not that I know."

The lioness walks towards a bubbling pot of green liquid, snapping pieces of cinnamon and shaking what appears to be lapis lazuli dust into it. "Good." She grabs a wooden ladle and puts it into the broth. She swirls it around, minding not to inhale too much of the vapour before lifting out a thick juice.

"Drink, Leandro."

Leandro stands, his face is scarred with scratches against his eyes, fresh ones. "And you are sure this will send me between our world and his?"

The lioness looks at him as she guides him towards the wooden ladle. "I'm most certain." The ladle is passed, and Leandro sits amongst the scattered cuts of Savannah grass that act as comfort for your feet on the ground of the hut and he props himself up against the wall as he begins to think back to that day it happened.

His might and will to live had outshone Koga's in the duel. A bittersweet victory, killing his friend sending him to the great plains. The chief had made him Zaffaza, to walk without Pride despite his words, stating that he fought like a coward and his next life may serve the Pride better than this one.

"I cannot help you if they find you here, you will be taken away in this state without any knowledge."

He looks to her through the dim light. "It's a risk I'm willing to take."

Leandro drinks from the spoon, ingesting this foul concoction. It squirms down his throat, scratching at the inside of his neck as it struggles down into his stomach, while he wretches. The fumes lighten the air as he pushes against the tent wall behind him struggling to see.

The room almost immediately fills with shadow, as the walls begin to become enveloped by a thick fog like darkness. His eyes close, succumbing to reality but reopen almost instantly. A void, of emptiness, beholds him. The floor is filled with a dark water, void of colour and only the shimmer of a shade of grey licks the outline of the distant pale structures that line the grim horizon.

"Brother?" Leandro calls out and waits.

"Brother?!" This time he shouts, saturating the air with an echo.

The echo returns and in the sound of Koga's voice, it repeats. "Brother."

From the shadow an orc walks through, he almost immediately begins to pace in a circle around Leandro. "Why do you come, Leandro?"

Leandro looks to his feet as he sighs. "I come because I am here to make amends."

Koga begins to laugh, releasing ripples into the water that seem to roll for miles into the horizon and noise that crescendos and reverberates at all angles.

"Brother, I wasn't like I was in life now that I am in death. Life is but the start of a long journey, one I now understand."

Leandro smiles as he looks to Koga. "And how is death? How are the plains?"

The orc shares his smile. "Magnificent."

His face becomes stern as he stops walking in circles. "Your story doesn't end here brother, there are so many moons you will see, so many people you will fight, so many will die at your feet."

Leandro's ears hear and listen carefully, concentrating intently on Koga's words.

"But that will not be your greatest accomplishment. That will be when you raise a small Zafrazzi child as your own. One that is on a journey to return home with unexpected guardians. One bold and one who is as strong as a hundred thousand Zafrazzi."

Koga's image begins to fade, as the water almost seems to consume his body slowly.

"What is their name? Where are they?" Leandro begins to run towards him, but the image does not seem to get any closer.

"That, brother, is something I cannot say."

Leandro charges as fast as he can, watching the water consume his brother.

"The path you choose now, will only lead to a single fate, one that is carved in stone, just like the others."

Leandro leaps, landing on where Koga was. The water had devoured his being in shadow and he watched the ripples erupt around him.

"Who else brother? Who else? What others do you speak of whose destiny is linked to mine?"

But the voices were gone, and nothingness settled in the In Between again.

Leandro woke, covered in sweat with bloodshot eyes and froth from his mouth.

"You were gone for a while Zaffaza. Daylight will be here soon." Said the lioness as she lifts up Leandro, wiping the drool away from his chin. "Did you find what you were searching for?"

Leandro was dazed, confused and tired. He struggled to his feet while his stomach still lay heavy. "I only gained more questions. But yes, I set things right. Thankyou Zi."

Zi lowers her head. "Now my debt has been paid for all the times you have brought me ingredients. Go, before you are found."

Leandro grabs his bag throwing it over his shoulder, and his hood over his head and mane.

"Walk with Pride Zi, I may see you in the next life."

"I hope you find the peace you seek, Zaffaza."

Leandro leaves the hut, and quietly runs out of the village, heading northwest.

The sun began to rise, leaving the two moons to settle, waving to its arrival. A single soul, alone, a shadow, a man with no pride, a Zaffaza walking the desert path, with no direction or plan ahead and no road to guide him.

For his life was forfeit for the Pride, for his life was nothing now. Yet, maybe, fate had a path and plan for him, just like Koga had said.

28

Arelle Goodsberry - Goodnight, Sweet Gesantia

Wind ripped through the burning towns and villages of Gesantia, whipping up the ash and settling it down on the blackened remains of buildings and people. But, on the edge of the kingdom, to the far south, the wind began to settle, and a spring air filled the lungs of all those who took in breath from it. An opening in between a large forest nestled in a glade, untouched by death and blood.

The border between Gesantia and the Kingdom of Inoria was a long line of farmland that stretched and weaved between forests and rivers. Migratory birds from the north live here, settling for warmer climate than the barrenness they once called home, enjoying feasts of salmon from the rivers and rodents from the forests.

Along a vast road of cobblestones and chiselled rocks was a line of refugees. Children huddle between their mothers, clinging to their legs for comfort or being held because of age, while the old hitch rides on the food wagons cuddled together for warmth. They had finished their long walk from their homes, tired, hungry, thirsty. Barely clinging on to their personalities, merely clinging onto the sliver of life they had left and just trying to survive.

Not a single person amongst them carried a weapon, nor plough or pitchfork. They were fatigued, tired of the fighting that raged across their country leaving desolation and destruction in its midst. Among the jaded there was one exception, a woman with a blade of a noble wrapped in cloth and twine saddled on her back while she held the child of an orc. She was not a fighter, nor was she a soldier's wife. She was young and she was bold.

Before these times, she would have been a topic of conversation, of question, of curiosity.

But not now. People didn't want to ask; these were dark days for all. There was something in her eyes that told them what they needed to know, and they didn't want to know the details of whatever she had been through.

They accepted each other as they were. Everyone in the line helped each other, when food was low, people shared, when people were cold, they gave warmth where they could. They were united in their displacement, showing a unity of equity.

Arelle carried Jay-Tor, swaddled in blankets and fur that wrapped around her body alleviating the weight of the now large baby orc. Remarkably, he had grown far more than a normal human would, five times that in fact. She felt that if she let him down, he would find his own way and walk beside her. She didn't dare try it, he was in her care, and she had come so far now.

"We will be there soon, little one, only a few more steps along this road."

Jay laughed, smiling uncontrollably at Arelle's speech. Giggling while he grasped his feet with his hands.

Along the road and over two bridges, towards the south, was the last bastion of hope for Gesantia and its people. A line of trenches in front of a palisade fort overlooking the north with large wooden stakes that line the edge of the wall. The fortification was situated within this glade, hidden from the fighting, hidden from the tremor of drums. It flew the Queen's banner high, and was a beacon for all that wished to seek refuge clear of the war.

It contained and mustered what little remained of the soldiers all those who hadn't been slaughtered, maimed or fled. This committed group symbolised strength and was joined by volunteers from all walks of life ready to do what they could while hoping that family and friends may walk along the bridges to greet them…

It was a flicker of hope, just enough that in the war-torn land, people had begun to flock there, camping in its belly or behind it in the woods.

An old lady looks down from a bread wagon, chewing on some food and knitting. "Everything okay dear? Are you hungry? How is the little one doing?"

Arelle takes her eyes from the palisade, meeting the gaze of the woman. The lady was old, frail with signs of cataract eyes and bruised dry legs hidden behind a tattered dress.

"Yes, thank you. The little one hasn't eaten yet today."

She breaks a piece off, offering it to Jay who accepts willingly as he shoves it into his hungry mouth.

"What's your name dear?"

The old lady asks patiently, continuing to knit as her eyes flicker between it and the conversation. She watches as Arelle bites down on the loaf. It was stale, but yet had a crusty shell, flaking off onto her clothes as she chewed upon a dry but moreish morsel.

"Arelle."

Spoken with her mouth full as the bread mopped up the remaining moisture in her dry mouth.

She finishes her portion.

"And you?"

The lady looks happily towards her, propping her knitting down.

"What a strong northern name! I had a daughter called Arelle."

She pauses, adjusting her dress.

"The pox got her though."

Arelle raises her brow and widens her closed mouth. "I'm sorry to hear that."

She looks down at Jay. He still had hold of his piece of bread, chewing on it like some fatty meat. He smiled when he noticed Arelle's face.

"My name is Meredith, and that's quite alright dear. It was many years ago now. Gods know she has probably walked the path without me at this rate. I've dodged death many times already. She's probably gotten bored and ran off."

Arelle doesn't respond, she only watches Jay's movements. His slight little kicks and thuds of play time.

"Is that little one yours? Aren't they a delight?"

And that indeed he was, she thought. He was cute, beyond belief, with two little tusks that stuck out from his mouth ever so slightly and great big eyes coloured like the brightest summer skies.

"No, his parents died in the war. I'm just caring for him for a while."

The old lady tuts her mouth, picking up her knitting as she begins to loop the wool between her needles. "My dear, that poor defenceless child looks to you now. They are more yours than their mother and father will ever be. Don't hide behind worry about what people think, sometimes it's best to accept fate."

Hopeful chatter begins to erupt from the refugees as the view of the palisade wall gets ever closer signalling that their journey across the entire Gesantian country in search of safety will come to an end.

"I made a promise to his father, that I would take him to his extended family. His place in life is not with us. It's with his kin. It's what his father wanted."

Meredith smiles. "Maybe you're right. But maybe he should be with someone who will keep him safe. So far you have done a fine job, accepting your guardianship and proven to be amazing at that responsibility."

Horsemen begin to approach the group, carrying banner flags of the Queens tower, they approach slowly as their horse's trot against the winding stone road, riding against the wind. Arelle looks, dazzled by the glare flickering from their armour as the sun beams down upon it.

They stop before the last bridge blocking the approaching refugees, manoeuvring their horses in front of them. There is some disgruntled muttering and concern amongst the group trying to guess what's happening. Arelle moves herself to the front, where many old men complain about the obvious attempt to thwart their journey, so close to its destination.

"We cannot accept any more civilians into the compound, we have barely enough food as it is."

Loud chatter erupts from the refugees. Some angry, some anxious.

"Maybe seek shelter in Inoria."

The crowds begin to build at front as discontent and obvious resentment starts to bubble within the group. A smell of ash and soot reeks the noses of all those who smell it, but most know it's probably their own scent. "It's another ten days trek before we reach a town in Inoria? We have barely any food left, and the water is beginning to wane. You are sending us to die!" a forthright member of the crowd spoke up, speaking on behalf of the others.

"I'm sorry, but we just can't help you. We have far too many mouths to feed and until a shipment of grain comes from the Queen, we won't be able to feed who we have for much longer either."

Arelle's gaze continues towards the palisade. Could she sneak in? At least then Jay could be safe for a while, they could fill up on food and then leave for Inoria in the morning regardless of the wishes of others.

A rider from the nearby forest begins to gallop frantically out approaching the fort. His head turns at each moment as he watches his back while his hand holds his reins and a horn. The horn sounds, ricocheting around the glade, startling the three horsemen guarding the bridge. They look to each other for comfort and then look back to the disgruntled crowds.

"What is that?" Arelle speaks out.

"Everyone must remain calm until we investigate."

Through the forest, three more horses' approach, one rider blows another horn, galloping frantically as he looks behind him. One lays back, lifeless as his body moves in a limp fashion. The other horse has no rider, but an arrow sticks from its leg.

"Rebels are coming!" A person from the crowd shouts.

"By the gods, I'm not standing around to die! Move out of my way!"

The horsemen resist at first but cannot suppress the force of the crowd that follows. They burst through squeezing past them as fast as they can, charging forwards with their children stampeding ahead with as much energy as they could muster from their heavily tolled reserves. The grasp of unity that they so needed at this time seemed to dissipate into the wind, as people fell from the rush, being trampled on leaving shattered arms and legs. It was fight or flight, and everyone had had enough of the fighting.

Arelle grasps Jay, who remains silent to all the commotion, absorbing the ambient energy of the crowd as it remains, still giving the same look he gave her the first time they met in the cave all those weeks ago. She holds him tightly against her chest and runs across the field towards the fort.

Gesantian was on its knees.

29

Lady Alayna Astravix - Into the Den of Lions

Katrina's chambers were triple the size of Alayna's bedroom and she had many personal maids that tended to her every need. As soon as they had arrived Katrina instructed that their attention was all on Alayna. There was no long wait for the bath to be drawn, as maids began turning the brass basin coil letting water rush in from the spring, heated up to a temperate feel from the heat of the sun. She was rushed into the room, undressed and brushed down before being helped into the basin which felt delicate and refined on the skin. Essential oils and rose petals were poured in, scenting the nose and tickling the bumps on the end of your skin heightening a sense of euphoria.

A while passed and she returned to Katrina's main chamber, fresh in body and mind, where the pampering continued. The maids had selected an array of exquisite gowns they thought would fit her and suit her colouring, while Katrina lit an incense stick which added to the ambience of the room.

Alayna was whisked off her feet, she started to think of her maids at home, how they had no smiles on their faces, how they were treated there. But it seems that in Katrina's room at least, the maids here were almost treated like family, sharing in the food and conversation. Martha would have loved it here.

" Nice bath?" Katrina enquiries too excited to wait for an answer. It wasn't often she had another younger lady to share style with. "I thought these would look nice on you, you can pick whatever one you would like … I think this one will be amazing on you."

Alayna is swept away in all the fuss, going along with Katina's recommendation, the maids help her into the dress and tugs at the lace at the back of her gown, tying it into a bow. Another has combed and started arranging her hair, while another has matched some jewellery and fastened it around her neck. They anointed her with rose oil and painted her face with special ointments and creams. They had to make do with shoes that were a little too big for her with a promise to have some made in the coming days with the finest of woven materials and prettiest of jewels.

"Well, sweetie, this looks to be a beautiful fit." Katrina smiles at Alayna through the long length mirror, something she had never had in Gesantia. Alayna looks into the reflected glass, and a wonderful image of purity shines back, light smacks against her reflection, dazzling the pearls around her neck and on her ears.

"Thank you, Katrina. This is just what I needed, and it means so much to me."

Katrina smiles, falling back towards the woven silk and feather recliner. "Did you have many fine gowns in Gesantia? These are the latest style fastenings, you look really good in this style, did you have any like this?"

Alayna pauses in thought thinking back to her gowns and the choosing day, her mother's anger and to poor Ezra and Martha. It was hard to believe it was only a month ago.

"I had some nice dresses, none this style though. My Mother was very particular and insistent on what I would wear."

Katrina toys with an olive in a nearby blue glass bowl before picking it up and putting it into her mouth. "Insistent? You make her sound so repulsive!"

Alayna doesn't respond, the maids are still fussing over her re-adjusting her jewellery, pinning her hair back with a silver pin. She sighs.

"What's wrong, pet?"

Katrina stands, watching Alayna's movements in the mirror as she walks over to loom above her shoulder.

"She… she was." Sweat begins to form in her brow as she continues talking.

"She was a very hard person to please and I couldn't do anything right. Everything she did was for some twisted reason. But she was my mother, and I don't know if she is dead or alive."

Katrina gasps. "Well sweetie, you won't be having any of that here."

Alayna's eyes meet Katrina's in the mirror. "I need to know what happened to her. She might come looking for me. And my father went to support the capital, how will he know where to find me? And what if the rebels come searching for me like they did Martha?"

"Don't trouble yourself with that today, Joseph and my father will get the answers as soon as they can. For now, you're safe here Alayna, nothing will hurt you while you are here with us." Katrina bends her knees going eye level with her.

"And if they try or even think about it. They would have to deal with the strongest armies Caldaria has ever seen. "She rubs her back.

"You worry over nothing honey. But if you ever need to talk or feel afraid about anything, I will always be here." For the first time, maybe in her entire life, Alayna felt secure. Martha has given her kindness, yes but didn't carry the power to make her feel safe. It may only last for this moment, but it was a feeling that came new to her.

"Come, they are waiting for us in the hall. I like being fashionably late most of the time, but I haven't seen my father in over eight months." She grasps Alayna's hand, prising her from the still fussing maids. "And he only comes to dinner when it's a special occasion."

Katrina extends her arm for Alayna to link, and they walk together, arms as one as if they were old friends. They step out of the marble bedroom and into the hall. It was filled with gold, with a trim that ran across the floor on either side. Great paintings of elven men and women, with pointed ears and pointed faces, adorn the walls and as they approached the bottom corridor the paintings started to show humans as Kings and Queens.

"Is there anything I need to know about formalities or that I should prepare for?"

Katrina rubs Alayna's hand. "What do you mean sweetie?"

"I was thinking of any special customs and how should I address your father? Also, if there is anything about your father, I should be aware of."

Katrina chuckles. "No, not really. He may seem a bit rough around the edges at times, but he means we'll. He always does."

They reach the hall main doors which are guarded by two very well armoured soldiers in a metal breastplate and chainmail.

"You'll be fine Alayna, stop worrying so much!"

The doors swing open and inside is the largest most majestic room Alayna had ever seen to grace the world. A huge painting governs the entire wall and ceiling, coloured and etched with perfect precision showing a great history of the empire the elves once had only to be finished by human hand at the back, showing their departure.

A grand table sits in the centre of the room, with silver plates and cutlery, candlesticks and large serving bowls covered to stop the insects from feasting. Around the table were six chairs and then another grander chair at the head of the table at the other end of the room. It was alone, secluded, in solitude from the other members of the family.

Joseph smiles as they walk in, standing up dressed in his ceremonial armour. His eyes follow Alayna's every move as he sits next to his younger sister, Gena, a well-mannered 15-year-old girl with black hair and a beautiful smile as she stands up holding Joseph's hand.

On the other side of the table are two empty seats and another girl, Joseph's youngest sister, Camilla, a 12 year old rascal who was playing with her toy dolls. Waiting for them at the door was an older lady, strong and fair with dark black hair, brown eyes and an eye shattering smile of delight.

"Welcome Alayna. Joseph told me about what happened, I trust you have been made comfortable in our care. You're delightful. Joseph, why didn't you tell me she was this beautiful. "

"I did mother."

"Oh, I just thought you were being you. You know what you're like with girls."

Alayna laughs nervously, blushing furiously while stealing glances at Joseph wondering who else he had talked to his mother about.

"It's a pleasure to meet you, your Grace." Alayna courtesies.

"And well mannered. You are right Joseph; she would make a good bride."

Now it was Joseph's turn to steal glances at Alayna, he didn't blush and only looked sheepishly as his mother gave his game away.

A slight pause between the conversation as a silence closes in. "Ma, where is pa?" Katrina looks to her mother inquisitively.

Joseph looks over. "He had some paperwork to fill out, he left this afternoon so should be here anytime now."

The empty chair at the end of the massive room anticipated their father's arrival.

Alone, with no cutlery, no plate or food nearby. The chair wad different to the others in shape and design with exquisite jewels crafted to make a spectacular design along the high back. Alayna only just had time to take in the grandeur of the chair, when the huge doors behind it began to open from both sides as a troop of soldiers lined up on either side letting in a hooded figure. Making sure to stay clear.

A soldier wearing all black steel steps forward. His armour was intricate and was fashioned with what appeared to be elf tear fragments around it that glowed a fabulous hue.

"All rise for his Majesty, Emperor Lucas, Second of his name and Imperial ward for the Elven Empire."

His body, from head to toe was covered in a pure white robe, and his face was obscured with a brass mask that concealed all his features. As he entered the room, all who were sitting, stood, even the little Camilla.

"Good evening children. Wife. "His eyes meet Alayna's.

"And Miss Astravix. It is a pleasure to meet you in person."

Alayna sheepishly stares and courtesies. "Likewise, your Grace."

He sits, with his hands between his legs at the other end of the table and only then do the other members of the family be seated. One by one, members of the court take seats and with-it Alayna follows, sitting next to Joseph and Gena, wishing Katrina had mentioned this custom.

"My deepest condolences to you. I only heard about the devastation your country had gone through merely a week ago. I hope the culprits are caught and dealt with appropriately."

Alayna sinks into her chair slightly but looks to the Emperor with a happy face. "Thank you, your Grace."

Maids and servants begin opening the silverware revealing beautiful cooked meats and spiced vegetables. The sweet smell of roasted pork with honey glaze, roasted potatoes with hints of salt and butter and various different types of vegetables.

"Come now Alayna, do tell me." He pauses, being passed a cup full of liquified food in a dish.

"What exactly are you doing in the city of two hearts?"

Alayna ignores the servant looking for guidance on how to fill her plate; she remains still, as the question petrifies her. "Your son. Your son saved me. Joseph saved my life."

Katrina nudges Joseph slyly, tilting her head towards her father and then turning to face him. Her eyes sharpen their gaze.

Joseph nods at her and then turns his attention to his father. "Father, now is not the time for questions. Alayna has been through enough? She has lost everyone and everything and you're questioning why she has sought refuge in our home?"

"No, it's quite okay, Joseph. I'm in your home, uninvited. Your father is trying to protect his family and his people. I get that. A few questions won't hurt."

Joseph turns to his father. "She's here because we intend to be engaged, father."

A shocked face rushes across all in the room and as Alayna turns her head to Joseph he looks at her with a similar distinction. The Emperor turns his head and two eyes beam through the eye slits of his metal mask.

"It was her choosing day and I had a hunch she was going to choose me, and I was totally bewitched by her" he said looking directly at her making her blush. "The rebels attacked, I went searching for her and saved her from a terrible fate. I decided to take her to safety here and along the long journey here we have become very close."

"Alayna, am I right? if so, let's make it official."

Alayna's confident facade crumbled at that moment, her young age, inexperience of social engagement and embarrassment of purity blushed scarlet on her face and made her voice fade and quiver "y, y, yes I would have chosen you, my father liked you and I would have declared myself a unity with you".

"You have no-one to announce to now Alayna - we can do that here together if you'd like" he said, holding her hand, coercing her to declare. She nodded and whispered the words that bound them "By my house of Astravix, in these unprecedented times..."

She looks to Joseph for emotional support, and he nods and then smiles.

"I Alayna of House Astravix declare a choosing with Prince Joseph of House Loredan."

"Then it's official we are engaged."

His mother, Maria, claps her hands. "That's wonderful news, isn't it Lucas?"

The metal mask shimmers the lit candles from the centre table as the Emperor tilts his head. "Splendid news. We had high hopes when Joseph decided to be presented at your choosing day. The union of our kingdoms is a most welcome outcome. Welcome to the family my dear." he raises an empty goblet in a toast and pretends to drink, as the family celebrates this news.

"Although unorthodox, with no family home I insist you have the wedding here. We can announce a day and invite the nobles here. I understand your father is supporting the capital of Gesantia, hopefully word will reach him, and he will join us. An honourable man and who I will pray for at the Cathedral later this evening."

"I am honoured by your gratitude, your Grace. Thank you so much." Alayna, shocked and dismayed, looks longingly at Joseph eyeing and blushes a red cheekful, eyeing up his posture and demeaner. He responds with a beaming smile and a very gentle kiss on her hand he has been holding all the while.

"Before I eat, I'd briefly like to speak with Joseph in private, there are some family matters to attend to, may you excuse us." Two guards walk over to the Emperor. Their arms are covered in a heavy coating of plate and cloth, and they use those arms to lift him from his seat.

Joseph stands to meet him, leaving the table and walking outside the doors his father came from. They clutch shut, echoing across the chambers with a loud thud. The guards then guide him down to a seating area overlooking the grand gardens and then they step back leaving them to talk in private. Emperor Lucas and Prince Joseph continue to converse in whispers.

"You have played your part well; she is besotted with you and you have led her to declare you as her choosing as we agreed."

Joseph grins.

"I have become a little fond of her, she is pleasant to look at, a little vulnerable and compliant so easy to get along with."

Joseph scratches his ear and looks into the gardens like his father.

"I also wanted to talk to you about Alayna's close miss with some of those rebels in Gesantia. The poor girl was nearly raped. The instruction was she was not to be harmed."

The Emperor nods.

"What's the issue? She's fine, isn't she?"

The Emperor looks to Joseph for a response before continuing with haste.

"It's all character-building Joseph, just like my illness."

Joseph looks to his father and looks to the locations where skin would be on show. His hands covered with gloves; his face covered with a mask.

"Have the researchers found anything from the elven archives?"

His father chuckles.

"My son." he pauses. "You know there is no cure."

Emperor Lucas looks at a painting on the wall of a young man with black hair on horseback.

"When I die, this kingdom will be yours. All of it. And when our plan begins to unfold, with Gesantia firmly under our wing like the old days of the empire we will finally rid the world of the republic and their heretical ways of the paths."

He turns to Joseph standing a good distance away. "I trust you have ordered a new shipment of elf's tears to be delivered to the Gesantian rebels? I've heard they will be assaulting the capital soon."

Joseph nods as he flicks his hair back and re-ties it into a ponytail."20 wagons full, about 100,000 gold pieces. The dwarven King was rubbing his hands I bet."

Lucas laughs. "I say that's a good investment into the security of our family. Well done my boy. Now let's put on our masks again and play happy little families. Then, you can go on with your little love affair."

Joseph smiles, reaching for the doors to open them.

"One more thing before we go in."

Joseph stops turning his head to his father's cold metal masked face.

"Rebel scouts report that Alayna's father was killed in action and Jezel was sighted entering the country of Evenstar, probably for a ferry back to the free lands."

Joseph nods, understanding its meaning. "Should I tell the girl about her father?"

"No, it's too soon. I will let you know when the time is right." The Emperor raises his fist in the air, gripping the pride that flourishes within him. "I have high hopes for this family. Don't screw up, you can still see your mistress even after you are married. I know a few spots where you could be discreet outside of the city."

Joseph stops at the door as he looks to his feet and sighs a deep, sensational one.

He then throws on a smile and flings the doors open to a chuckling group sitting at the table.

There, Alayna smiled, joking with the women and girls who made idle chatter, starting on planning details for the wedding. The Prince's glare was met by two mesmerising blue eyes which seemed to begin dreaming. Dreaming of a future that she was so desperate to have, dreaming of a family, a life, of friends of a loving husband.

The Irony was that those around her were going to sap her soul more than her mother ever did. She was easy to manipulate, so desperate for affection and needed to be loved. She couldn't see they only wanted what they could gain from being with her.

But she was the happiest she had ever been.

30

Arelle Goodsberry - Re-Awakening an Act of Balance

In eye distance, from within the forest, a large army breaks through the treeline. It was fragmented, like peasants would be, but a formidable force of strong men, enough men to outnumber Gesantians troops five to one. They bear weapons now, weapons of steel, of point, of sharp edge. Treasures of war looted from the bodies of all those who stood in their way.

Arelle charges past the horsemen, gripping baby Jay in her arms tightly as the linen and leather wraps firmly around her. She held him close to her chest, making sure to hide his face from the oncoming onslaught. The rest of the refugees begin to follow, running for the cover of the trenches and the palisade wall.

"Stay close little one, stay close."

Teary eyed and full of adrenaline, Arelle makes good haste, separating herself from most of the group who stagger behind whether that be due to age or frailness. The screaming begins at first, with very little view on what is going on, Arelle at first thinks it's frustration at getting so far and being blocked to enter by the horsemen until she sees a large group of rebels are heading their way towards them.

A galloping of hooves takes off from behind her, she looks over her head, continuing to run as she does. The horsemen blocking the road now swiftly move past the fleeting refugees towards the safety of the palisade.

"Cowards," Arelle said under her breath, continuing to carry her feet.

The wind broke, and then a whistle of what sounds like migratory birds can be heard above. She thinks nothing of it, stamping through the grass as fast as she could watching the hastier refugees in front make good time. But those were not birds.

Arrows begin to splinter in the floor, embedding themselves into the dirt and then into the women and children who had made good time. Arelle drops her head, falling to the ground holding baby jay as tightly as she could shielding him with her own body. The impaling continues as outside of her protective cocoon, screaming is heard peppered into the dominant noise of whimpering, crying and moaning.

She cannot risk helping them, she needed to keep focussed on getting to safety with Jay. There was little time. When the whistling sound stops, Arelle lifts her eyes up to the horizon, seeing the devastation of life all around her...

She was still for a moment as the entire world stopped. Children grip their mothers attempting to drag them across the floor with wounds that rival many, while mother's weep for their babies which are unable to move as they rock back and forth on the floor trying to breathe life into them once more. She looked down at Jay, who looked at her like it was the first time they met. Still breathing with her in unison, keeping her in check.

A charge is sounded, and the entire column of rebels descends upon the refugee line screaming "Fuck the Queen" as they raise their cold steel into the air.

Arelle reacts swiftly, collecting her sense and continuing her flight. She makes good ground, running with all her strength jumping into the trenches on the far side, not threatened as yet from the onslaught. Behind her, many follow her lead, seeking refuge in a group rather than to run out alone into the open.

Soldiers in chainmail bearing the symbol of the Queen's spire on their tabards wielding spears and shields charge past her, making their way to the front line to die. One stops, turning his head noticing the party of women, children and the old.

He breathes heavily with panic in his eyes. "What are you doing here?" He stops. looking at crying babies and mother's covered in blood.

"There is an opening in the trenches. Down this tunnel and under the hilltop. You need to be quick as we will be getting ready to barricade it as quickly as possible. I suggest trying your luck in the forest. I don't think we are going to beat them." He points towards the walls, and inside the tunnels is an opening where light shines from flickers of torchlight.

She thanks him and bolts forward cutting across a crossroad of tunnels making her way past sleeping posts and dirty water that sits in pools of mud and muck underneath the wooden supports. Rats run through the water, eating at anything edible they find on the way, gnawing at the framework for sips of moisture that isn't covered in filth.

Explosions then begin from behind her as blue flames light up the refugee line, murderous noises begin and with it does the clashing of swords upon the screams of many. The smell of fear and death, as some wet themselves just before the stench of their blood fills the air. It intensifies for a moment, with what little resistance the old and young can give them. Then, maybe even more horrifying, the sound of silence follows as the grimness of short life from the refugee line is cut short.

Meredith climbs down into the trenches, breathing heavily as each breath leaves harder than the first. Her hand clasps her neck which produces heavy amounts of blood tainted by a stain of a bluish tint. It was inevitable that she would join her daughter today. But there was no time to talk, there was no time to help. They had to press on.

The tunnel was held up by makeshift wooden frames perking up the mouth of the tunnel with a struggle. The group pushed inside, being forced to walk in a singular line down narrow corridors surrounded by earth as the sound of war rages above them.

The ground and cave walls shook, as elf tears are being used as exploding ammunition that crashes into the walls and into the ground above them. Dust from the ceiling falls, shaking the sconces and lanterns.

Arelle pushes the group forward, using her left hand to feel the walls to guide her path, while struggling with the weight and wriggling of Jay, who was scared and crying. The diminished line of people following her now holding onto the person in front trying to guide each other through the darkness. But then, they hear a scream from inside the tunnel echo its way down the darkness, and know the rebels are following their path, killing those they find on the way.

Another volley of elf tears land, snapping behind them, breaking through the ground above and into the wooden supports erupting the hilltop into itself. There were no words for the cries they heard, as fellow refugees were crushed under the weight and rubble.

Arelle counts her blessing and continues on her quest, not faltering, pushing inwards with what little of the group remains as they squeeze out of the tunnels and into the fort's courtyard.

There, they run towards the edge of the wall, pressed as far away from the front gatehouse as possible, hiding with the other men and women who do not bear arms and only watch the onslaught in front of them. A Well Wood tree sits in the centre of the courtyard, covered in flags and symbols, offerings to the gods and letters to fallen family and friends.

Many people brace the main gate, some soldiers, some guards, some untrained and unknowing people from all backgrounds unlucky enough to stumble here as everyone tries to stop the end from approaching ever quicker.

The door slams, sending the people bracing it flying backwards, others quickly come forward becoming human barricades as they give what resistance they can and push back, slamming themselves this side of the wall. It slams again, this time splintering some of the wood revealing some of the horrors that await them.

Gesantian soldiers take aim, firing their crossbows through slits, catching some of the aggressors with steel bolts, while some cast their spears through the holes piercing any stupid bastard who even tries to get this close. And then all hell breaks loose.

A catapult from outside the city flings its contents. Most of it cascades, catching the walls erupting into blue flames. But a single elf tear lands in the centre courtyard, exploding near the Well Wood tree.

Arelle is thrown into the air and is slammed into the wooden wall behind her. Her hands become limp, and she drops Jay to the ground before landing to cold stone herself.

Through the searing light and piercing ring in her ears, one thought burns brighter than the flames. Her legs won't respond, so she claws her way forward, fingernails breaking against stone, each inch gained a victory of maternal desperation. The world slowly comes into focus – but she wishes it hadn't.

The courtyard has become hell. The air fills with the screams of the mutilated and dying, but Arelle hears nothing except the terrible silence from the small bundle ahead. No precious giggles. No hungry cries. No sounds of the baby boy who had been laughing in her arms mere moments ago.

Terror claws at her throat as she drags herself to him. "Please," she whispers, then louder, "Please!" Her trembling hands reach for his tiny chest, searching for the flutter of a heartbeat that has marked every peaceful night since she was graced with his presence. There is only stillness.

"JAY!" The scream tears from her soul, a primal sound that joins the chorus of suffering around her. Her eyes stab wildly around, seeking help from the survivors, but each is trapped in their own private horror. "Please, someone! My baby – help my baby!"

She gathers him close, her tears falling on his peaceful face. This can't be real. He was just smiling, just reaching for her hair with those perfect tiny fingers. The battle rages at the gates, but for Arelle, the world has already ended.

A gentle touch on her shoulder. Through tear-blurred eyes, she sees a figure wrapped in layered cloth, one-armed, face hidden beneath a hood. She recoils instinctively, then sees something in his bearing that speaks of healing. Hope flares painfully in her chest as she forces herself to let go, to give this stranger room to reach her child.

He kneels down and looks to her red eyes flooding with tears. She quickly noted the man was wearing many clothes that covered his skin, he had only one arm, and carried no weapon with him. She moves back to give him some room, crying out in pain while pushing the dirt behind her to give herself some leverage.

He placed his hand onto Jay's chest and breathed heavily through his mouth and in through his nose.

The main gate slams again, catching Arelle's attention. A brutish laugh challenges many behind the wall, as an axe smashes against the wood and crushes someone from the other side. She turns back to the man and Jay.

Blue energy begins to flow from the stranger's hand as he focuses on every ounce of thought and moment in what he's doing. A thick sickly smelling cloud of haze rushes over Jay, entering his nose, ears and mouth clinging to his flesh and lungs rushing into his blood and nerves.

Jay begins to cough, and the energy then flows to another dead refugee or Gesantian, and then to another until all those who had fallen nearby from the elf tears now breathe life again.

"Thank you. Thank you so much." Arelle's voice breaks, tears welling in her eyes as relief floods through her body. She reaches toward the stranger with trembling fingers but stops short of touching him, overwhelmed by what she's witnessed. Then her attention shifts to the baby orc, its tiny face hooked in fear, fat tears streaming down its greenish cheeks. Without thinking, she kneels beside the infant, her own tears now falling freely. "Shh, little one," she whispers while gently brushing her fingertips across the baby's forehead. The child's cries soften slightly at her touch, their shared vulnerability forming a bridge between two worlds that were never meant to understand each other.

The battlefield smells burnt the nostrils and lungs, filling it with uneasy breaths of heavy toxic smoke. The stranger walks to Arelle and pulls Osric's sword from her back before rushing towards the gate.

The wood smashes again, but this time it erupts sending splintered wood everywhere revealing hundreds of rebels eager to murder. The Gesantian forces retreat further into the courtyard, gripping their weapons and forming up behind the Well Wood tree for a last stand, clinging to the thought that every kill they make will be justice for Gesantia, justice for their families.

The rebels follow, screaming and cutting down all who are too slow to the mark before stopping at the sight of the clothed man, with one arm and a blade in his hand. He stands ready, with a tainted blue in his eyes that sickeningly clouds his iris. He lowers his hood and cloth mask from his face breathing in the tainted air that poisoned the sky.

The brutish man sporting a brown beard from the rebels walks forward shocked beyond all belief. He carried an axe, and a sword in his belt. "It can't be …. Saracen Murdock."

He smiles and begins to clap, displaying his scarred arm. "I get to kill you a second time. You impress me but unfortunately, today you and your people will rot in the dirt becoming feasts for the maggots. Just like the day I left you in the dirt all those days ago."

The Gesantian forces cowered, looking at whoever was left, forming a small shield wall to protect the women and children. Maybe fifty or so live, but only a few have the strength to hold their shield high enough to help.

Saracen's eyes begin to glow, pulsing with energy as he stares towards the rebels that have amassed themselves in front of him.

"No, today is not our day. Today, Gesantia will live again, breathe, love, laugh, play, and sing songs of the defiance we caused in stopping you here. Today, you will become ghosts, walking the Well Wood paths as souls without purposes and minds lost to illness and festering in your own thoughts."

The brute laughs, catching a Gesantian trying to crawl away from the corner of his eyes, caving in his skull with his axe.

"This one is mine, the rest…."

He rips his axe from the skull, detaching the head from the body and tossing it behind.

"Make them a feast for the crows."

He raises his axe into the air and begins to advance with the rebels screaming behind him charging forwards.

Saracen's eyes begin to loom, as the very earth and rock from underneath his feet and around him deform, disintegrating into small stones while dust begins to lift into the air, glistening from the charge of the blue energy.

He looks to the Gesantian men behind him, erupting his sword into blue flames and his eyes begin to glow a bluish haze that flows like rivers down his cheeks and onto his chest. They look in awe, as their hearts begin to fill with courage watching the Well Wood tree begin to glow in unison with Saracen, the magic that resonates from within his eyes, like two hearts beating in rhythm.

Saracen then lifts his sword in the air, and the men begin to form up around him.

"For Gesantia!"

31

Sir Osric Erenbell - The Tipping of the Scales

The tipping point between conscious reality and the world we create while unconscious was difficult to decipher. He didn't remember the journey or the voices that dragged him out of water and across the snow, it was only a hazy memory that taunted him, a shadowy veil thrown over his whole person before he succumbed to an unconscious state stumbling into the dreamlands.

He was walking along a path lit up by the overwhelming light of a Well Wood tree, the largest one he had ever seen that seemed to reach up beyond the clouds and into the ether of darkness above. Along this road were many people, talking to him as if he was an old friend, holding each other's hands as they stopped at nothing to keep moving but he had no recognition of them. They were of all races, of all colour and gender… But, among them, he saw Arelle, who smiled at his sight.

She looked along the road, pointing out to a young woman with fiery ginger hair, grasping a wooden stick. He focuses in, squinting his tired old eyes along the road to meet hers as she stares back.

"Wake up…."

An echo erupts into a roar, cascading reality and unmaking it like shattered glass. He falls, watching the others continue their journey along the long road towards the tree above him and he closes his eyes.

His vision began to flicker open back to reality, hearing voices talking from all around him. He was startled at first, realising that his whole body was numb other than his neck. His memory still dazed and hazy managed to piece together past events that when he pushed Arelle to sea, the third bolt ripped through his spine. He was paralysed.

His head lay on a hard surface and as he looked to his right, he realised he was in fact laying on top of a table and there, sitting with a grin on his face, was the Baron.

"My goodness Sir Osric, you're awake. Thank you for choosing the perfect time." The smile returns to the Baron's face as he sits drooling over a bowl of nuts.

One of the many voices from behind him begins to speak. It was deep and booming, one that could fill any space with resonance.

"Anyways, we return to the matter at hand. The shipment of elf tears from Astronozia is arriving at the front lines in four weeks. This gives us some time to prepare, gather troops, train them, and pick a few more to enhance my Lord. Then we can carefully plan the assault leading up to the elf tear arrivals closer to the time. "

The Baron's glare turns to where the voice is coming from. "Good! And what of your plans to liberate that ghastly city of yours? Astronozia's King seems to think he owns all of Caldaria, I can smell his arrogance from a mile off."

The voice laughs.

"We have certain preparations in place. The Prince plans to marry a Gesantian girl who managed to escape from the south. Their illegitimate relationship will surely cause difficulties in court when brought to its attention. I doubt that the Arudanian politicians will appreciate a Gesantian Princess in their palace and eventually a Gesantian Queen ruling them. They have far to much pride for that."

The Baron impatiently awaits more.

"Well, is that it?"

"No. The Prince has a concubine, may I suggest we use one of our three children to infect her as she will be a remarkable spy."

The Baron nods in approval.

"Also, our efforts in court have allowed us leadership over certain aspects of the city. Here."

A hand reaches over, passing the Baron a scroll with a wax seal. He pops it open and unrolls it to see the contents.

"Very good, very good indeed."

He rolls it back up and tosses it.

"And what of you?"

The Baron looks over Osric's head to another who sits around the table.

"We have tried all our experiments to see if the other species can be accommodating hosts. However, we have concluded that out of all the creatures in the world with a brain large enough to accept it, Humans are the only ones without magical interference."

The Baron nods.

"Yes, I had high hopes for the orcs, my experiments with an orc female lead to no leads. But, well done for your effort."

The Baron stands, rustling in a chest behind him and produces a small wooden container. He places it onto the table.

"And so, we have a plan going forward, the necessary steps have been put into place for a total annexation of the Western front. In a month's time, I want to hear exactly what we plan to do with the east and beyond."

He looks to Osric, lapping at his lips like a dog to a finished meal, wiping the morsels from his mouth.

"When we have liberated the capital city from the Queen, I will bring forth a new kingdom. One that will be the foundations to a new world."

He delays a smile before looking down to the little box, slowly opening it.

"The Astronozians will be too busy killing each other to notice their promised lands are forfeit and by that time, our plans will have enveloped anyway, liberating them from their shallow lives."

A grubby hand reaches into the box and pulls out what appears to be a small insect. It attempts to escape with all its strength, struggling to reach for the flesh of Osric pulling with all its might against the pinch of the Baron.

"You're wasting good babies on someone who cannot walk, or swing his sword. He is of no use to us."

The Baron laughs and smiles with vigour, staring at the sound of the booming voice.

Osric could only stare, his mind screaming out as much as he could, but his pride told him to remain silent.

"This is Sir Osric, the famous knight of the order. The one who has many years of experience."

The Baron pauses and looks back at him while snapping teeth as he manoeuvres the insect over Osric's face.

"And hidden knowledge that will assist us in our plans."

He lifts up from the table, peering over Osrics body, grasping hold of the creature with one hand.

The insect drops landing on Osric. He struggles at first, trying to move his weak head from left to right. The creature was a warped grotesque mess of wrapped black appendages, eyes that gaze in all directions and scorpion like tail on its back. It sits on his face, imbedding its poisonous tail into his skin injecting vile venomous sap that seeps into his blood, intoxicating his body with an eery cold feeling.

It scurries up his cheek, with sharp mandibles that snap as they get close. Its stomach was bloated, with little black balls that hang like fruit from a tree, unfertilised eggs waiting for seed to hatch inside an unsuspecting victim. It drools at the sight of him, dripping hot salivary streaks of wet drips that stick like webs on his face. It scurries over his mouth and then grabs hold of the edge of his nose with its legs and appendages.

Osric Tries to shake his neck but he cannot move. He is screaming inside but cannot maneuver the muscles in his face to form the sound. His last moving parts now useless with powerful venom.

The bug then squeezes into his nostril, and he feels it push through the soft flesh, making room as it enters deeper into the cavity. It starts to stretch its way through, and then he feels sharp pains in his head as it becomes overwhelmingly difficult to keep his eyes open.

The pain, unbearable to think of, as it feels as if his mind breaks into pieces, and he begins shaking in a fit like state. But, almost as quickly as it started, the shaking stops. Osric could see through his eyes. But he could not feel anything, he could not move, he could not talk.

"Sir Osric?"

The Baron looks over with curiosity.

"Are you with us? Did it work?"

Osric's head turns.

"Yes."

He could see the Baron smiling. But he did not move his head, he did not utter breath or talk.

Something was pulling at his strings, he was the puppet and the insect was his puppeteer. The Baron sits, sighing relief as he pats the paralysed torso of Osric. He then lifts his hand away, reaching for a nearby crystal vase, pouring himself and the others a glass of whiskey.

"Tell us…."

The glass, swerling in his hands, surveying the room with his predator eyes before looking towards Osric. The glass lifts to his mouth, opening widely to allow the liquor to fall onto his tongue, revealing small termite like creatures that have imbedded themselves to the inside of his mouth, and a larger beetle rooted on the roof of his mouth.

"…Everything"

Epilogue

Many miles away, in a hollow, deep within the dirt of the good earth is a burrow torn into the ground that etches it's way through the rocky pebbles and gritty mud, beneath the Veil of burrowed creatures beyond the naked eyes of this world. Within the confines of the burrow are shelves brimming with books and other educational implements that line the scratchy wooden furniture adding to the scenery of scattered candles with half burnt wicks. Unfinished, bookmarked tomes lay open at specific pages, dusty to the naked eye and lay scattered through its dimly lit halls. The burrow carried the comforting aroma of a long-lost home, where the rich, savory scent of bubbling vegetable stew intertwined with the earthy scent of old books and tattered wooden furniture that warms the torchlight.

Within the room furthest from the main entrance was a dark gloom shaken by the tickle of a sickly blue flame that projected flashes of imagery within its cold ember. Stood next too it, studying its movements while crouched over like an arch was a mouse the size of a man, smothered in a blue robe that was tattered at his bare feet. His eyes watched with awe as his hands flick to the side replaying the imagery that lay in front of him for the countless time.

——————

"For Gesantia!"

Saracen charges forwards with the other soldiers at his sides as they face the hordes of rebels who aim to end the war.

He swishes his wrist, breaking the barrier between reality and magic, as a wave of heavy sickly smoke pushes out from his hand and into the approaching rebels front line.

It enters their lungs, giving no remorse or prisoner, wrapping its dense foam like texture within their bodies dropping them to the floor as they splutter pellets of fluidy bile grabbing at their throats, clawing at them to release what they just inhaled. The soldiers behind them topple over their bodies and the charge loses momentum as it smashes against the ground like waves against a rocky cliff.

The Gesantians waste no time, stepping forwards as a body, as one unit, casting their spears and their blades into all those who fell, feeding their steel with the blood of all those who took the lives of their families. But Saracen watched forward, letting the magic sink from his fingertips and bubble underneath his skin as it began to turn grey. From within the hordes of enemies, a large brute of a man, the one who removed Saracens arm from his body, holds his hand over his mouth shielding it from the smoke as he clambers over his fallen comrades gripping a blood stained axe in his hand and wearing a horrible glare over his face as they share a glance at each other.

The brute charges, stepping onto his fallen men, crushing ribs and bones along the way before leaping towards him.

He swings his weapon, smashing it into shields, cracking them behind his weight as his drool fills his mouth.

Saracens hand casts out into the air, catching the brutes essence in his grasp as if he was a puppet while his body remains perfectly still and only the flick of his eyes manoeuvre there way around the battlefield in shock.

For the first time, Saracen sees fear in this man, as his eyes loosen their hunter-like gaze. The other rebels also stop, watching their commander spin and turn towards them, as the puppeteer tightens his grip on his strings.

Saracen steps forward, still keeping a hold of the brute with his mind as he looks out to the other rebels and watching their every move.

"Your peace, your sickened justice, comes to a striking end today."

The brute's hand snaps and a groan awakens from his mouth while the other rebels watch in fear.

"How can you live with yourselves? For all of the children and innocent people you have murdered?"

He lifts his hand in the air and then burns a hot blue flame in between his fingers while looking onwards towards the enemy. They then watch the brutes head snap backwards, crushing under the weight of a thousand horses as it cascades into the dirt behind him. His back begins bending backwards, crunching and breaking like twigs upon an Autumn walk, crushing into a pulpy mess before being tossed aside like refuse.

And then, the rebels, freeze in fear with eyes of terror, the same eyes they have of all those who were cut down in their blood lust.

Saracen, stares into each and everyone of those eyes, picturing the horrors they committed and the rage that has consumed them, blinding them into a sense of justice. But, he just clenches his first tighter, stepping forward onto the bodies that lay gasping for breath below him, while he inhales deeply.

He fought to steady his thoughts, but rage swallowed him whole. A fury born of vengeance. A fury ignited by fate.

That day, the Well Wood Trees shone a little brighter. They twinkled in the night to follow. For the souls that they laid claim to were guided the onslaught that Saracen gave them. The beaten earth lay darkened with blood, like rain sinking into parched soil.

Gesantia fled into the shadows. Waiting in the dark to fight another day.

———————————-

The mouse pauses the imagery, moving the palm of his hand over the elf tear that emits its magic as he looks towards the still picture of Saracen with puzzled eyes and a heavy frown across his face.

He grabs a twisted wooden staff balancing his weight onto it and then takes the elf tear that shines on the pedestal and places it back on top of the stick.

Walking towards a bookshelf he let's his hairy, boney fingers scratch against the book covers as his eyes follow the trail, examining the spines of the novels and guides that clutch against each other like lost scared lambs, hoping that their fates are not shared with the other neglected pieces of knowledge that line the furniture outside of the bookcase.

"No no, not these, not these ones."

His eyes cast against the open pages of others that cross his path, gaining an insight to past reads before his attention turns elsewhere.

He takes his stick and swiftly turns to walk towards a closed chest that hides underneath a rag of stitched clothes that have been cast over it.

He glares with discontent, as his brow closes loosely over his eyes.

Lifting the cloth from the chest, the mouse also reaches from underneath his robes and tugs on a key held together with twine around his neck.

He takes a step back and using his staff, glows the elf tear attached on top to move the key into the clasp and breathes a heavy sigh before opening it.

The chest snaps open, relieving the rusty lock of its job that barely held its confines together, flinging the lid backwards revealing an array of black leathered tomes of old with elven scriptures on. Ones that hallow the mind even thinking of what they utter within their words.

He lowers himself to the ground, glowing the elf tear crystal above so that it makes the symbols clearer to the eye, revealing dancing motes of light that lift from the dark cover. A sense of decay begins to ravage the air.

His hand hovers over the top, as dark words echo in his ears, feasting on his thoughts to what ungodly scriptures lay in front of him.

The Mouse stops, his eyes fixate on a particular spine tucked underneath the vast majority of the others as he shudders at the text it mutters. He reaches down to pick it up, brushing the spine and front cover with his hand before putting it in his large pockets.

Lifting himself up with his stick, the mouse leans against it for support before walking towards the rooms exit passing all those books he had opened before.

The hallway it led too was well structured, with wooden flooring and rustic wooden beams that hold the earth from toppling on his head. It was a makeshift construction, one that was added to over many years and one that adorned ornaments and notes that hang from bent nails or shoddy hooks.

He lowers his head before tucking under a low beam that leads into a messy kitchen that still bubbles a broth of vegetables over a fire. Sage and other cooking herbs line the ceiling, hanging dry and crooked and the centre of the room lay a table with two empty chairs and then a third chair with another mouse sat on it.

"You startled me, Whiskers. Is everything alright?"

Whiskers looks horrifyingly towards the other, holding up his staff to glare the blue light towards his eyes.

"Night is falling upon our merry rock, the sun that once shone brightly will soon fade and the light will die to the shadow. I think its time we began preparations, Rakasha."

She lays down her book and removes her glasses from her snout before looking up to him.

"Your reciting the prophecy Whiskers? What signs have been given to you?"

Whiskers scratches his face and snout as he begins to pace back and forth.

"I have seen in the magic Rakasha, humanities grasp on the in between has begun. It is as the prophecy foretells. "

Rakasha stands as her hands tremble.

"What are we to do? "

Whiskers, concerningly nods as he looks to the exit and begins to walk towards it.

"We will speak to Tyria, and see if she feels or sees anything...."

Whiskers stops, and looks back to Rakasha, almost snapping his neck as she watches him stutter his words. Fear taints his expression, something that she had not seen since the elves left Caldaria.

"... The Reckoning is upon us."

The Adventure will continue in book 2: The Watchers in the West.

www.ingramcontent.com/pod-product-compliance
Lightning Source LLC
Chambersburg PA
CBHW020249030826
48979CB00030B/2760/J